AUTHOR'S NOTE

The following story was originally written in 1998 & 1999 as a six part series of short stories. Each part was always meant to be the final part but I always ended up writing another sequel.

The downside of this was that there were a few small glitches between parts, so in 2003 the six stories were re-written into a five part larger story so that they could run more smoothly into each other.

PART 1

2001

NICHOLSON RESIDENCE

EDINBURGH

21:47

James Black sat inside of the car, parked across the street from Sally Nicholson's house. He'd been sitting in the car for the last three and a half hours since he'd followed Sally home from work. It wasn't that he didn't know where Sally lived but instead it was part of the fun.

He'd waited three years for this and now that it was so close, it seemed a shame to rush it. He got out of the car, stretching slightly before starting to walk slowly towards the house. He knew that she was alone in the house. Her boyfriend hadn't turned up tonight. That was one of the reasons that James had waited. He wanted to make sure of what he was up against. The boyfriend's presence wouldn't have stopped him but it would have made him alter his plans slightly.

Inside of the house, Sally Nicholson turned off the T.V. set and got up to get ready for bed. She'd had a hard day at work, plus she had to get up fairly early tomorrow for another day at work. No rest for the wicked, she thought to herself.

She switched off the living room lights and headed up the stairs towards the bathroom. Her intention was to have a relaxing bath before heading to bed. She always slept better after having a bath before hand, hell sometimes she caught herself starting to drift to sleep during the bath itself.

Outside, in her back garden, James watched as the bathroom light came on. He stood watching her through the frosted glass window, as she got undressed. After a few minutes of this, he walked over to her back door. He didn't really think that she would be stupid enough to leave it unlocked, but he tried it anyway. Just as he'd thought, it was locked.

He moved over to the drainpipe. On a previous visit, earlier on in the day, he'd already established that the drainpipe was made out of metal and not plastic, as seemed to be the way these days.

Once satisfied that he had a good grip on the pipe, James began to pull himself upwards slowly but surely until he was level with the bedroom window. Like her routine had suggested, the window was opened almost as soon as she got back from work. Sally didn't like sleeping in a stuffy room, or so it would seem.

Using his left hand and his feet to support himself, James reached inside of the window with his right hand. Gripping the plastic security catch, that stopped the window from being opened further than it should, he started to pull. With little effort the snib on the catch snapped and the window swung wide open. James began to pull himself into the house over the window sill.

In the bathroom, Sally was now soaking in a relaxing bubble filled bath. The woes of the day slowly leaving her body and she was starting to doze off, when she was startled by a thump from the direction of her bedroom across the hallway. She lurched upwards, causing the water to slosh over the sides of the bath, the bubbles riding on the surface of the water.

Inside of Sally's bedroom, James reached down to his side and pulled a large knife from its sheath on his belt. He started across the room and into the hallway.

Sally was by this point out of the bath and into her dressing robe. She had her ear pressed up against the door listening for any more sounds. After five minutes of listening and not hearing anything, she unlocked the bathroom door and gradually began to open it. Peeking out of the gap into the hallway, she couldn't see anything out of place. She waited another few minutes before opening the door fully and stepping out, completely unprotected. The light from the bathroom was flooding through the doorway into the shadowy hallway corridor.

The upstairs of Sally's house had three rooms. Sally's bedroom, the bathroom and at the far end of the hallway was the spare bedroom. It was in the darkness of the spare bedroom that James stood watching as Sally entered the hallway from the bathroom. His right hand still gripped the knife at his side, his knuckles white from the strength of his grip.

Sally stood in the hallway for a second, listening. She was starting to have doubts as to whether or not she'd heard anything at all. Maybe it was her imagination. After all she had been on the verge of falling asleep in the bath. One way or the other, the only way to find out was to check the other upstairs rooms. With that in mind, she started to head off in the direction of her bedroom.

She reached her room and flicked the light switch on. Instantly the room was illuminated and on a first glance nothing seemed out of place, but just as she was about to convince herself that she had imagined the thump, she noticed that the window was swinging freely. That wasn't right. She'd left it on the catch as she always did when she got in from work. She walked across the room, the breeze from the open window feeling cold on her skin, especially after her bath. So much for the bath sending her to sleep, she thought bitterly. Halfway across the room she stopped, her gaze having just settled on something lying on her carpet. What was that?

Moving closer to the item to try and work out what it was exactly, Sally suddenly felt a chill right through her whole body as realisation of what the item on the floor was and what it had to mean swept over her. Her breath caught in her throat and she stepped backwards, pulling her dressing robe tighter against her as if to shield herself.

The item on the floor was the catch to her window and for it to have been snapped off like that, it could only mean one thing. Someone had broken into her home, while she had been in the bath. The thump, her mind screamed at her. Oh God, the thump. That was what had gotten her out of the bath in the first place and worst of all that meant the intruder was still in her house.

Fear instantly grabbed her and she started to back out of the room. Once in the hall she turned and raced to the stairs. She had to get out of the house and call the police. Tearing down the stairs, two at a time, she lost her footing, in her haste to get to the bottom. Pitching head first down the stairs, Sally toppled down the rest of the way down to the bottom.

A little dazed from the fall, Sally took a second to recollect herself. She then started to push herself back up with her hands, a shearing pain shot through her ankle when she started to put her weight on it.

Shit, she thought to herself. She must have twisted it in the fall. She would have to look at that later, she had to get out. Wincing through the pain, Sally continued to get herself back to her feet.

James had watched Sally run for the stairs from his vantage point and had heard the noise as she had fallen. He began to move out from his hiding place, his adrenaline racing at the thought of finally being able to get even, of finally beginning the steps of getting his revenge. He reached the top of the staircase in time to see Sally reach her front door and began making his way down the stairs himself.

Sally was just grabbing hold of the front door handle when she heard the heavy sound of footsteps on the stairs behind her. Despite her fear, she felt herself turning round to face the intruder. She saw him approaching the halfway point of the stairs. He was dressed in black, about six feet tall with dark brown hair. In his hand she saw a knife. But that wasn't what caused Sally to catch her breath again, what really got her the most was when she saw the intruder's face and recognised who it was.

'No,' she muttered, the blood draining from her face. 'No, you're dead.'

James stopped on the stairs, enjoying her obvious fear and shock that he was still alive. He tilted his head slightly, a small smile playing on his lips.

'Apparently not,' he replied.

Sally turned back to the door, gripping the handle and turning it to get out. James was on the move again as well, closing the gap between them, fast.

Although it turned, the handle didn't give any and the door refused to budge. Come on, Sally thought to herself. What was wrong with it? Then it dawned on her. In her panic, Sally had forgotten that she'd locked the door before going up the stairs for her bath.

'Shit,' she cried out as she realised her mistake. Grabbing the key and turning it, she heard the heavy clunk as the lock turned. Pulling on the handle, she finally got the door open, but didn't even get a foot outside before she was grabbed by the throat and hauled back into the hallway.

James threw Sally to the floor, before turning and slamming the front door closed. Sally started to cry with fear. She knew what was coming and worse still she knew that there was nothing that she could do to stop it.

'No, please don't,' she begged. As useless as it was to try and reason with this man, she had to try.

James grabbed her again and pulled her back up to her feet. Pushing her against the wall, he moved his face in closer so that it was almost touching Sally's.

'Did you really think that this was over? That you could really get away from me?' he asked. 'I've waited three years for this. Three long years and now your time is up.'

'No. Please,' Sally continued to beg. 'I don't want to die.'

In one final attempt to break free from her attacker, Sally started to kick out at her him, but to no effect. Continuing to pin her against the wall with his left hand, James pulled the knife back with his right. Then with a completely expressionless face he plunged the blade into his victim's stomach.

Sally cried out in pain and tried to double over, but James still held his grip on her and wouldn't let her move more than a few centimetres. Blood had begun to ooze out from around the embedded knife, staining her dressing robe crimson. James gave the knife a clockwise twist and wrenched it to the side, opening the wound even further. The wider gash in Sally's stomach caused the blood from the wound to start dripping on the carpet, pooling around her naked feet.

He pulled the knife out and released his grip on Sally, taking a step back as he did so. She fell to her hands and knees. With tears running down her face and whimpers of pain from her mouth, Sally started to crawl away in a feeble gesture of defiance. The blood was starting to leave a trail as she continued to crawl away towards her front door, her robe undone and hanging open as she made her struggle for freedom and safety.

James stood watching for a few seconds, enjoying the sight of Sally's pain. He let her crawl so far before stepping up beside her. He raised the knife up high and brought it down hard into Sally's back. The blade grated against one of Sally's ribs as he pushed it in deeper.

Crying out, Sally collapsed onto her front. The pain finally causing her to lapse into unconsciousness. James frowned slightly at this. He wasn't at all pleased that his prey wasn't conscious any more. Fun and games were over then.

Reaching down with his left hand, he grabbed Sally's hair and pulled her head back, exposing her throat. With his right hand, he brought the knife round and sliced her throat open. Releasing his grip on her hair, her head fell back down to the floor with a thud. Within seconds her face was lying in an expanding pool of blood.

He stood above for a few minutes, watching her as her life's blood left her body, before bending down and wiping the blade of his knife on her dressing robe. Once satisfied that the knife was clean enough, he re-sheathed it.

Reaching into his back pocket, he pulled out a photograph of a man and a woman at the supermarket. It was time to announce to the world that he was still alive. He dropped the photo onto the floor a little away from the body but not so that it wasn't obvious that it was from him. With that done, he turned round and left the house leaving the front door wide open. Seconds later, he had disappeared into the night, leaving the car across the road for the police to have as well.

NICHOLSON RESIDENCE

23:33

Detective Frank Thorn stood looking down at the blood stained floor in the hallway of Sally Nicholson's house. Her body had been removed not long ago. He had seen brutal murders before, but it never failed to make him wonder how anyone could do this to someone else. The forensics team were going through the scene with a fine toothcomb. In theory Frank shouldn't even be at the crime scene at the moment. He was technically contaminating the scene. The only reason that he was here at all was that the photo found at the scene had bearing on him. It was a picture of himself and his wife, Catherine. Worse still, it was a recent picture as Catherine's hair in the photo was short and it had only been cut two weeks earlier. Before then it had been half way down her back.

This would have been cause for concern at the best of times, but the choice of victim killed tonight made things worse because the two events were a message and he knew exactly what it was saying.

He turned round and left the house. He had to speak to his superior, Carl Pullman. He had the photograph in a sealed plastic bag in his pocket. He got into his car and drove off.

LOTHIAN AND BORDERS POLICE STATION
EDINBURGH

00:01

Carl Pullman was just getting up from his desk with the intention of going home. He had been trying to leave for nearly three and a half hours but something kept coming up. He grabbed his jacket from the coat hook on the back of his office door, started to put it on when his door opened without even so much as a courtesy knock. Detective Frank Thorn entered.

'I need to speak with you,' Frank started. 'Its very important and it can't wait until tomorrow.'

'I've heard this from you before Frank, and every time without fail, it hasn't been as important as you've made out. In fact the only person that it has been important to has been you.'

Frank ignored this comment and pressed on regardless. He and Carl didn't always see eye to eye, but there was a level of professional respect between them, regardless of how pissed off Carl sounded now.

'You've heard of James Black?' Frank asked.

'Yeah. He was a serial killer some years back. It was before my time here though, but as I recall he was killed.'

'Correction,' Frank interrupted. 'Presumed killed. His body was never found.'

'Excuse my lack of details,' Carl retorted. 'Like I said I wasn't here at the time. I was still down south. I just remember reading about it in the news. What has this got to do with what you want to see me about anyway?'

'It would be easier if I filled you in on the specifics of the Black case first. Three years ago the Edinburgh area was hit by a spree of apparently motiveless murders. He just killed for the sheer hell of it. There was no pattern. Men, women, young, old, black and white. It didn't matter to him. Once he had decided on his course of action, you were as good as dead.

'The man you replaced two years ago, Robert Platt, put me in charge of trying to catch the man responsible. The murders continued and evidence mounted up, but despite having fingerprints, hair and fibre as well as various other bit of forensic evidence we were never able to identify the perpetrator. As time went by the killer became surer of himself until at the last murder site he left his name scrolled in the victim's blood on the wall. That name was James Black. Even with his name, the only thing we could find was a school registration form and it was so long ago that the address on the form no longer existed.

'We had only one more chance from that last murder. There had been three victims that night and one survivor. The survivor gave us an artist impression that we were able to show on the news, with a hotline set up.

'A few days later we got lucky and a woman phoned in to say that she had served the man in the picture at the bank she worked at. The bank security tapes confirmed that she was telling the truth. We had hoped for another name from the account he was using, but no such luck. He was only getting change of a ten-pound note. We put an undercover officer in the bank in the hope that he would come in again. Two days later he did. He bypassed the shorter lines for service to wait specifically for the woman who had contacted us in the first place.

'Unfortunately, we didn't have enough officers at the time to make the arrest, and he was gone by the time back up arrived. It did allow us to learn that he seemed very interested in our female informant. I felt that it was safe to assume that she was likely to be the next target.

'After securing Robert Platt's permission and the woman's cooperation we set a trap for him using the woman as live bait. Less than a week later, he struck and despite our fairly large presence, not only did he almost kill her, but he got away again. We thought that we had lost our best chance, but we got sight of him heading in the direction of the Forth Road Bridge. We knew that once he got to the other side of the bridge we were screwed as we didn't have time to go through the proper channels to make the arrest outside of our jurisdiction.

'When our units got there he was halfway over and had grabbed a four year old boy from his mother. He was using the boy as a human shield, a knife pressed up against the boy's throat. Robert Platt, who was by this stage in a fairly unstable emotional state after the death of his wife ordered police sniper, David Walker to take aim and fire.

'The bullet hit James square in the chest. The impact knocked him off his feet and over the railing of the bridge. Unfortunately he pulled the boy with him. Both landed in the sea below and although we were able to recover the body of the boy, we never found James Black's body. Despite my protests, James was listed as dead and the case was closed.'

'After a bullet in the chest, a fall from the road bridge as well as having to swim in the sea whilst bleeding, I would think that it was a fairly reasonable conclusion to come to that he was dead,' Carl replied.

'Besides if he was alive where has he been all these years? In fact why are you telling me any of this in the first place?'

'I'm telling you this,' Frank returned trying to control his anxiety, 'because tonight James Black finally came out of hiding. I've just come from the house of a woman named Sally Nicholson. She was killed tonight and I'm telling you that he was responsible. Her killer was James Black.'

Carl paused for a second, trying to suss out how serious Frank was before replying. 'Even if James Black was alive and well, what makes this murder so special that you just know it was him?'

'Sally Nicholson was the woman who contacted us three years ago and the woman we used for bait.'

This finally grabbed Carl's full attention although he was still reluctant to fully believe what Frank was telling him. 'Coincidence,' he voiced cautiously.

'That was my first thought,' Frank replied. 'Until I saw this.' He pulled the photo out of his jacket pocket and handed it to Carl. 'It's a message. He's telling us that the murder is no coincidence and that it isn't over yet.'

Carl looked at the photo of Frank and his wife, pondering over everything that he had just been told.

'Okay,' he said. 'Assuming that you are right and James Black is alive, what can we do to catch him? Bearing in mind that you couldn't do it three years ago.'

'We have certain advantages now that we didn't have three years ago. For example we know what he looks like and the fact that he has come for Sally suggests to me that he is after revenge for those that hurt him back in '98.'

'You think that you can guess the targets?' Carl asked.

'I think that there are four obvious choices for him to go to. Four people that were involved in his downfall three years ago. Sally was the bait and now she's dead. There was Robert Platt who ordered the sniper, David Walker to shoot, but Robert died several months ago in a retirement home.

The sniper himself would seem like an obvious target and the final target would probably be me as I headed up the investigation and I masterminded the plan to try and trap him. The photo found with Sally's body would seem to back this guess up.'

'So what do you suggest we do then?'

'Talk to the sniper, David Walker. Warn him about what might be about to happen. Put an unmarked car outside of his house. Have the police officers report in every hour. I can take care of myself, but while I'm here I'd appreciate a patrol car to be put outside of my house to ensure that my wife is safe.'

'All right. I'll assume that you're right. You'll get you're cars for now, but I better see some results.'

'Thank you,' Frank replied, before turning to go back out of the office, leaving Carl with his own thoughts.

Frank moved down the police station corridor with a purpose, playing over everything that he had learned tonight. Part of him still didn't want to believe that James was back after all of these years, but deep down he knew that it was really happening all over again.

'Please God,' he muttered to himself. 'Help me to stop him once and for all.'

WALKER RESIDENCE
EDINBURGH

09:11

David Walker stood at the front door, watching as Detective Frank Thorn left. He had come to warn him that both he and his family were in danger. David closed the door and started to head back into the house.

'What was that all about?' his wife Tina asked from the kitchen.

'Nothing,' he replied. He didn't see any point in worrying his wife with what may or may not happen.

His mind wandered back to that night three years ago on the Forth Road Bridge. He remembered the man in question. He also remembered that he had hit the target square in the chest. By his reckoning, the target should have been dead before he even hit the water, especially after falling over the railing.

Of course, he had felt very guilty about the little boy dying in the process. He still did. He hadn't banked on James pulling the boy with him.

Nearly every day since then he had wondered what he would have done if it had been his son Eric. He constantly felt responsible for the kid's death. He had spent months in therapy as a result of that night. Even now all these years later, that nagging feeling of 'what if' haunted him.

He had left the police force shortly after that night. The job just didn't appeal to him any more. He was trying to put all that behind him and he had almost succeeded, until now.

Now all these years later, the past was coming back to get him in the form of the man that had caused all of his problems anyway. The question he had to ask himself was this. Did he really believe that James Black had survived?

The answer, he decided was no, not really. Yes, Sally Nicholson was dead and the killer seemed to have something about Frank Thorn, but that didn't mean it was anything other than a copycat killer.

There was nothing at the crime scene to suggest that he was in any danger. Maybe on the other hand he was just trying to deny what was right in front of him. Maybe he just didn't have the nerve to face the truth.

Either way, he decided to stay quiet and not tell his family. He didn't believe that he was in any real danger. Even if James Black was still alive, there was a police car out front. He wasn't likely to get past that.

The police car did create a problem however if his wife noticed. Then he would have to explain himself. Even though it was unmarked, it didn't take a rocket scientist to work out that it wasn't visitors to the neighbourhood, especially since they didn't get out of the car very often. The only time would really be at shift change.

Still he would keep quiet and cross the bridge with the police car if and when his wife noticed it. With his mind made up, he made his way through to the kitchen to eat his breakfast.

MALCOM RESIDENCE

TWO DAYS LATER

22:49

James stood by the window, watching the unmarked police car across the street. He had been watching for the last fifteen and a half hours. Watching their routine. Of course he had expected Frank to send an unmarked car to the Walker house, and as predicted it had turned up. No doubt the Walker family had been warned as well. Not that any of that mattered.

He turned to look at the dead bodies of the old couple that had lived in the house. They weren't of any importance to his plan, but he needed a vantage point where he could watch both the Walker residence and police car and their house was directly across the street. Unfortunately for them when he broke in, they put up a struggle, and now they were dead.

He glanced at his watch. Nearly eleven o'clock, and the officers in the car to make their latest report. As a result it was almost time for him to make his move. He reached down and started to pick up the plastic green fuel cans that he had brought into the house. He would need them later. Each can held just over five litres of petrol and he had a total of four.

WALKER RESIDENCE

23:08

James stood in the shadows of David Walker's only son's bedroom. The seven-year-old lay sound asleep, oblivious to what was about to happen to him. Security in the house was a joke, especially for a family that had been warned that their lives were in danger. It had taken him all of two minutes to pick their back door lock, and no alarm system. In this day and age he was very surprised, but it made his job much easier. He pulled his mind back to the job in hand.

He pulled his knife out of the sheath and started to move across the room. The boy turned slightly in his sleep. James paused at the side of the bed, the knife in his right hand poised to strike. He reached out with his left hand and clamped it over the kid's mouth so that he couldn't scream out. The boy's eyes opened immediately, a look of panic in his face. He started to struggle against his attacker, but couldn't even come close to overpowering a fully-grown man.

James raised the knife and brought it down full force into the boy's chest. The impact caused the blade to burst through not only skin and flesh but also several ribs. The killer pulled the knife back out, the blade catching on the rib fragments as it came free. Raising the knife back up again, James brought the blade down again, and again, and again, until the body of the boy was nothing more than a bloody mess.

23:27

James now entered the master bedroom, where both David walker and his wife Tina Walker were sleeping. In his hands he had cradled the dead body of their son. There was a trail of blood from the son's room across the hall to the master bedroom and James himself was covered in blood. His knife was back in its' sheath for now, but he could get it out at a seconds notice.

Hoisting the body above his head, James launched it at the sleeping couple. It hit the bed, face down, the peach sheets becoming stained as the boy's blood ran out on to them.

The couple woke with a start at the impact of something hitting them. David pulled himself into a sitting position.

'What the hell?' he muttered, not seeing what had been thrown at them but instead at the figure of James in the doorway. He realised at this point that he had been wrong to dismiss Frank Thorn's warning. This was when Tina realised what had been thrown at them.

'Oh God,' she cried. 'Eric, No.' she turned the body over and started to cradle it in her arms, oblivious to the blood that she was getting on her naked arms.

'Eric,' James said with a smile. 'So that was his name.'

Hearing his wife's distress, David turned to see what the issue was; finally registering what had been thrown at them. After the initial shock, his first reaction was anger.

'YOU SON OF A BITCH,' he shouted as he pulled himself out of his bed and lunged across the room at the intruder. James sidestepped and lashed out with his fist. He connected with David's chin, which sent the ex-sniper crashing into a dresser unit at the side of the wall.

James moved up to him and kicked him in the side. David doubled up with the impact, his ribs cracked by the blow. Satisfied that David was of no immediate threat, James turned his attention to Tina, who was still holding her dead son and crying. She hadn't even noticed that her husband had left her side and been attacked.

Moving over towards her, James pulled his knife free yet again. Once level with her, he grabbed her by the hair, pulling her head back and exposing her neck. With one fluid movement he slashed her throat open. Within seconds, her life's blood joined that of her dead son's.

David was on his knees by this point, struggling against the pain in his sides in an effort to get to his wife.

'TINA,' he called out. 'You bastard. I'll kill you.'

Despite the threat, he was barely on his feet when James grabbed him and pushed him against the wall, the killer's right hand holding him by the throat.

'You couldn't kill me before. What makes you think that you can kill me now?'

David struggled against the grip of his attacker, but the more that he struggled the tighter the grip around his throat got, until he was having serious difficulty breathing. He started to gasp in desperation for air.

'You caused me a lot of pain three years ago and I wanted to do the same to you. This is why I couldn't kill you until I had made sure that you knew that everyone that you care about was dead. Now that is done, it is you're time to die.'

With that he tightened his grip and David's throat. Squeezing the air out of him, until the inevitable happened. Minutes later, he threw the body to the floor, like a rag doll.

James glanced at his watch. He was running out of time. He had to get the rest of his plan ready in time for what he thought Frank would do next.

LOTHIAN AND BORDERS POLICE STATION

00:06

Frank sat in his office, trying once more to get into the head of this serial killer that he had hoped and prayed was dead. Was it too obvious to assume that he would go for either himself or David Walker? Is that what the killer wanted him to think or was James really going to go for revenge? To make matters worse, the lack of leads on this case was meaning that the cars he had watching both his own house and that of David walker were being questioned. The longer it took for James to surface, the harder it was for him to justify the use of the cars. He was distracted from his thoughts by a knock at his office door.

'Yeah,' he called out.

The door opened and a young officer entered. Frank recognised him as Officer Roberts.

'Sir,' Officer Roberts started. 'The officers watching the Walker house haven't radioed in for their midnight report and they aren't replying to our attempts to reach them.'

Frank was up in a second, knowing right away that he had been right and exactly where James was. 'You're coming with me,' he ordered.

WALKER RESIDENCE

00:10

James threw the last of the now empty fuel cans to the bottom of the stairs where the other three had also been discarded. The trap was set. He had splashed petrol around every possible exit downstairs, the smell was intoxicating, but it would also work for him as well.

00:17

Frank slammed the radio in the car back down. He had just made yet another request for back up but had been told that the nearest unit was fifteen minutes from the Walker house. Both he and Officer Roberts were in a police car hurtling towards the Walker's as fast as they could. Officer Roberts at the wheel, looking slightly nervous, glanced back at Frank.

'What do we do?' he asked his superior.

'It's just you and me for the next quarter of an hour. Stay alert. If you make any mistakes with this guy, it'll cost you your life.'

He reached into his jacket and pulled out a gun, checking to make sure it was loaded.

WALKER RESIDENCE

00:18

James stood at the window in the master bedroom. It looked out on to the Walker's front garden and allowed him a view to watch the road. In his hand he was holding a gun which he had found and taken from a desk drawer in David's study. In his shirt pocket, lying against his chest he had a lighter, ready for when he would need it. After three long years, his revenge would finally be complete.

Not since he was a teenager, had anyone hurt him the way that these people had. Not only hurting him but stopping and almost killing him. He remembered clearly the fateful night where it had all started to go wrong. None of that mattered now however. After three long years of waiting and biding his time, he was finally ready to reveal that he was alive and soon his reign of death and destruction would resume properly where he had left off.

00:22

The police car came to a screeching halt beside the unmarked car and Frank leapt out, his first thought to check on the officers inside. Reaching the car, he opened the door and the body of one of the officer's fell out onto the pavement, his throat gouged open. The other officer lay slumped against the door on the other side. His neck had been broken. How James had been able to overpower both of them without attracting any attention was beyond Frank.

'Come on,' Frank called out to Officer Roberts, who was just getting out of the car himself, looking like he wanted to be anywhere else but here. Normally Frank would have pitied him, but he didn't have time tonight.

James Black was a highly dangerous man and Frank needed what little help he had.

Frank started to head off over the lawn towards the front door, which he just bet would be conveniently unlocked. Officer Roberts was behind him. Abruptly the silence was shattered by a gunshot.

'Shit,' Frank muttered. 'TAKE COVER,' he ordered Officer Roberts, turning around as he did to check on him.

What he found was Officer Roberts lying on his back sprawled out on the lawn, with a pool of blood expanding from his shattered skull.

'You son of a bitch,' Frank hissed through clenched teeth. 'So, just you and me then. If that's how you want it. Let's do this.'

Holding his gun tightly in his hand, he stood up and marched the last few feet towards the front door. If James had wanted him dead, he could have shot him like Officer Roberts. It looked like James wanted to play games.

He reached the door and turned the handle. Just like he had thought, the door opened without any effort. He pushed it open and entered cautiously; the smell of petrol hit him in the face instantly. Seconds later, his eyes fell onto the fuel cans lying in a discarded pile. Back out, Frank's rational side said to him. If this isn't a trap, what is? Despite this, he found himself still moving further into the house.

James watched from upstairs as Frank entered. He watched the Detective start to move to check the downstairs rooms. Reaching into his shirt pocket, James pulled out the lighter. He flipped the metal lid open, revealing the wick, his thumb resting on the roller wheel that would light it up. He threw the gun down to the floor. It was no longer needed.

'FRANK THORN,' he called out. 'LONG TIME, NO SEE.'

Frank spun round at the sound of the voice. Seeing James standing at the top of the stairs, he started to head towards him, his gun raised and pointing towards his enemy. The vapour from all of the petrol was starting to seriously sting his eyes but he continued forward anyway.

'NOT SO FAST,' James shouted, holding the lighter up where Frank could see it. Frank stopped, fully aware that the house was a rigged firetrap.

James smiled. 'Well done,' he said, his voice taking on a remarkable calm sound. In his hand he flicked the roller and the spark ignited the wick on the lighter. Frank almost called out in protest at the madness of this action. Half expecting the house to go sky high, but nothing happened, despite the vapour level in the house.

James himself had felt a moment's nerve as he had lit up the lighter. He had done his homework though. He knew that petrol vapour was heavier than air and as such the highest quantities of the vapour would be on the ground level of the house and thus it was Frank that was in the most danger – or he would be in a few seconds.

Frank stood at the bottom of the stairs, glaring up at James. He put his foot on the bottom stair to start climbing up them, to reach his goal.

The killer's response to this was to throw the lit lighter over Frank's head towards the front door.

'NO,' Frank called out, but it was too late. The lighter hit the door, the flame catching an area that James had rigged earlier. The vapour went up and a small inferno began, following the path of the petrol that had been splashed over the place.

Quickly the fire spread, eating the furniture as it went. Flames encircled the doorway and smoke began to rise to the ceiling.

'COME ON DETECTIVE,' James called out. 'COME UP AND FACE ME. LET'S FINISH THIS OFF ONCE AND FOR ALL.'

With that James stepped back from the top of the stairs, disappearing into the rising smoke. Frank was torn. He wanted to follow but he knew that he might not be able to get back out of the house if he put off escaping whilst he still could. A few seconds later, Frank made his decision, despite the flames and the smoke, Frank had to give pursuit, if for no other reason than, more innocent people would die if this madman wasn't caught. He started to climb the stairs two at a time.

Back downstairs the fire had encircled the electrical fuse box, which finally exploded under the heat of the flames. The power in the house was lost and the only light came from the rapidly growing flames.

Upstairs, Frank pushed open the first door he came to. From the poor light he could only make out that it was a child's room. The Walker's son, Eric, probably. The light coloured bed sheets were stained a dark colour with what Frank felt was safe too assume was blood. Sick bastard, he thought.

Outside the house, the first of the back up cars arrived. The police officers inside got out in time to see the downstairs living room windows shatter outwards as the fire intensified and spread even further. The officer nearest the car reached back inside of it and radioed for the fire brigade and an ambulance, whilst the other officer started to evacuate the next-door neighbours.

Back inside, James watched as Frank headed towards the master bedroom. He pulled his knife from its sheath and lunged out of the shadows towards his prey.

Sensing, more than hearing him, Frank spun round to face James, raising his gun and firing as he did so. James was too fast and too close however and the bullet whistled past him. The killer plunged the knife into Frank's stomach, twisting it as he did so. Crying out in pain, Frank lashed out at James, his fist catching the killer in the face, knocking him backwards.

James lost his grip on the knife as he fell back. Frank collapsed to his knees as the pain of the knife wound got to him further. His grip on his gun lost, it too fell to the floor. The fire had reached the upstairs landing and was spreading fast, the smoke almost a solid wall in the poor light.

Downstairs the flames had reached the gas boiler. It was only a matter of time before the inevitable happened.

James straightened himself up from the blow and moved back in towards Frank. Frank saw him coming and tried to get back to his feet, but James kicked him in the side, knocking him back over.

Reaching down, James clamped his hands onto Frank's head and started to crush. Frank tried to struggle but his blood loss coupled with the smoke was making him weak. He felt the pain as James pushed his thumbs against his temples, pressing harder and harder. His vision began to blur and he found it increasingly difficult to focus or struggle. His hands began groping around for anything and came across his fallen gun. Grasping it in his right hand, he raised it and fired blindly. Almost instantly he heard a howl of pain, followed by the pressure on his head stopping.

Frank raised his head again, his vision slowly coming back. He could just see James against the far wall, clutching his leg. He didn't have much time. He struggled back to his feet, ignoring the pain in his stomach, the knife still embedded. His eyes were watering from all the smoke and he was having trouble breathing. Staggering into the master bedroom, he found the corpses of David, Tina and Eric but he was too preoccupied to think much of it.

James saw Frank making his way into the bedroom and ignoring his own pain, straightened up to follow. Downstairs the gas boiler finally blew and the house shook with the force of the explosion. The ceiling directly above the boiler, already weakened from the fire, gave way and started to collapse.

Upstairs, both James and Frank felt the force of the explosion, unfortunately for James he was directly above the boiler and when the floor started to collapse it took him with it. Despite his attempts to find a handhold to pull himself up, he disappeared into the inferno below.

In the master bedroom, Frank reached the window, raised the gun and fired again. The glass shattered and Frank started to move forward to haul himself out. The window ledge hit the knife handle sending an arrow of pain through Frank. Too make matters worse the glass shards from the broken window were also digging into him as he pulled himself outside.

By this point, outside there were several police cars, an ambulance and a crowd of curious people. Two fire engines had just arrived and were getting their hoses set up in an effort to control and extinguish the fire. Frank's appearance at the window had gotten everyone's attention. Firemen quickly started to get ladders ready to try and get to him.

On the outside window ledge, Frank hung on to the windowsill to stop himself from falling. He was feeling incredibly dizzy and could just make out the firemen trying to reach him.

What he didn't see as a result of his back being turned to the window was movement from inside of the master bedroom. James had made his way back up the stairs, completely oblivious to the fact that he was alight. His mind set on reaching Frank before he could escape.

Suddenly a fiery arm burst out from behind Frank, grabbing hold of his jacket and trying to pull him back into the house. Frank's jacket caught light and he lost his grip on the windowsill as he struggled against his attacker.

With his grip on the windowsill gone Frank toppled forward. James leaned out of the window trying to stop it but Frank slid out of his jacket and fell to the ground below. He landed on his front, the impact of the landing hammering the knife further into his stomach.

There was another explosion from the house and a fireball raged through. James disappeared from sight in the flames. Minutes later the roof began to cave in and the flames shot skyward.

On the lawn below, paramedics were attending to Frank trying desperately to save his life. Frank had by this point slipped into unconsciousness, which the medics thought was probably for the best as they weren't hopeful at all.

LOTHIAN AND BORDERS POLICE STATION

THREE DAYS LATER

10:10

Carl Pullman sat at his desk with a copy of a provisional report concerning the incident at the Walker's house three days ago. There had only been three bodies recovered from the blaze. Those of David Walker, his wife Tina Walker and their son Eric walker. There was no sign of James Black's body. Normally he would have said that it was impossible for anyone to have survived that fire, but the police had assumed that James Black had died before and it had cost lives.

The total death toll still wasn't clear as Frank Thorn was in critical condition at the hospital. He still hadn't regained consciousness yet and the doctors weren't sure when, if at all, he would.

Without a body, Carl decided that he had to assume that James was still alive and if he was that meant that Frank was still in danger. He'd spoken to Frank's wife Catherine about the possible threat still hanging over Frank's life and they had reached a decision about what to do.

Later on today, he would issue a statement saying that Detective Frank Thorn had died in hospital and would be buried next week. They would even stage a funeral with an empty coffin so that if James was alive and watching he would believe that Frank really was dead and thus give some breathing time to work out how to proceed.

If it turned out that James really was dead then they could easily let it be known that Frank was still alive.

If however, James really was alive then Carl had decided to take control of the case personally. He just hoped to God that the sick son of a bitch was burning in hell somewhere.

PART 2

ONE WEEK LATER

10:47

James Black stood in the distance, amongst the gravestones, watching the service as Frank's coffin was lowered into the ground. Frank had been a worthy opponent and the taste of victory was almost bitter sweet.

He looked down at his hands, which were badly burnt, from the house fire the previous week. His own trap had almost cost him his life. As it was he had barely escaped.

What was puzzling him slightly was the speed with which his body was healing. Still that worked in his favour. Now that his revenge was complete it was time to revert back to his motiveless murders like he used to do three years earlier. Certainly the randomness of his crime when he did that was part of the appeal.

In the distance, he could see Frank's wife Catherine, dressed in black, standing by the graveside. He could also see what he assumed were undercover police officers. If this was the case, then the police obviously didn't believe that he was dead.

He turned and headed off in the direction of the exit. He had work to do. He'd already selected his next victim. A woman named Lucy Tomrie. He'd seen her as he had been driving around. Already he had discovered her name, address and was starting to piece together her routine. It was now just a matter of choosing his moment.

He reached the car that he was using at the moment. He'd stolen it, just a few hours ago from a supermarket car park. He would have to dump it soon otherwise he'd run the risk of being picked up by the police.

Getting inside of the car he started the engine and drove off. The police would soon have their confirmation that he had survived the house fire.

LOTHIAN AND BORDERS POLICE STATION

19:27

Detective John Carter was standing in the office of his boss, Carl Pullman. He had just come from the cemetery, where there had been a police presence all day. They had been looking for James Black, but so far hadn't had any luck.

John personally didn't believe that James Black was alive. He thought that it was impossible for any one to have survived the type of fire that James had been exposed to, but Carl Pullman insisted that until they had some sort of evidence that James was dead, they had to assume that he was still alive.

John was in his early thirties and had a good reputation in the department, but he was not very patient and his patience with this saga was wearing very thin. The only thing that held his tongue in check was that he had a respect for the chain of command and if Carl said “jump”, he would ask how high. He frowned on mavericks like Detective Frank Thorn and despite how good Frank had been at his job, he couldn’t condone the risks, his results took to achieve.

Carl turned round to face John. ‘Still nothing?’ he asked.

‘Sir,’ John agreed. ‘With all due respect sir, I think that we are wasting time and money. There is no way that James Black could have survived that fire. It is probably only a matter of time before his body turns up.’

‘Well until it does I want everyone to assume that he is alive. If it were anyone else, I would agree with you. When Detective Thorn came to see me, I didn’t really believe what he had to say, but I gave in to get an easy life. He turned out to be right and it cost lives that no one believed him from the start. I won’t make that mistake again.’

Resigned to the fact that Carl wasn’t going to back down, John turned back to the business in hand.

‘Okay,’ he said. ‘How do we capture him? If he is alive, that is. There was no sign of him at the funeral, but that doesn’t mean he wasn’t there. He could have been in disguise or watching from a distance.’

‘I don’t know,’ Carl admitted. ‘I just don’t know.’

TOMRIE RESIDENCE

THREE WEEKS LATER

22:03

Lucy was dozing in her chair. She had had a long day and was tired. She was twenty-eight with long brown hair, blue eyes and a really friendly nature. She was single at the moment and her life literally consisted of getting up, going to work, coming home, eating and sleeping. The only real company she had was her dog Max, whom she had to leave in the house whilst she was out at work.

It was this dog that woke her up from her snooze. Max knew his routine, and he knew that he was overdue for his night walk. He started pawing at Lucy’s leg in an effort to wake her up. A few minutes later she roused herself from her sleep and after getting her bearings again, she checked her watch.

‘Shit,’ she muttered. ‘Is that the time?’

Lucy stumbled to her feet. She was usually back from taking Max out by half nine. She was running very late. Max gave a small bark at seeing his mistress get up of the chair.

‘Yes, Max,’ she said to the dog. ‘I see you. Come on.’

She grabbed his leash from the living room table and clipped it on to Max's collar. The dog was practically dragging her to the front door. She got out, turned and locked the door, all the while with Max, straining at the leash.

This was going to have to be a quick walk, she had to get to her bed otherwise she would never get up in the morning. She started heading down the pavement, stopping now and then so that Max could do his business.

James watched her from across the street. He was standing at a bus stop so that he didn't look suspicious.

'Little late tonight aren't we?' he muttered to no one in particular.

Stepping off the pavement, he started to follow Lucy at a distance, his hand reached down to his belt where he had his knife in a sheath. His fingers were idly playing with the handle.

The first drops of rain started to fall from the night sky and Lucy cursed and about turned to head back to her house. Max's walk would have to be cut short. She started jogging back home, completely ignoring the approaching figure. Max was barking playfully as he kept pace with her. The rain meant absolutely nothing to him.

James saw her turn back towards him but continued onwards anyway. If only she knew that death was coming for her, then maybe she wouldn't be as quick to run straight towards it. He picked up pace as they were almost about to pass each other.

Lucy was passing the oncoming man, who seemed to not care about the fact that rain had started and was getting heavier. He didn't even have a coat. Still that wasn't her problem. Out of the corner of her eye, she could see that he was playing with something on his belt, but she couldn't make out what. Before she could see what it was, she was past him.

James continued walking on, letting her live for now. The time wasn't right. She would die tonight, but not here. He turned the corner of the street so that he was out of sight of Lucy, should she look back over her shoulder.

Waiting fifteen minutes in the rain, to give her enough time to get back inside of her house, he too about turned and started to head off back towards his prey.

22:49

Inside of her house, Lucy was upstairs in her bathroom, getting dried off and ready for bed. Max was downstairs eating. She slipped into her nightgown and left the bathroom for her bedroom across the hall.

Downstairs Max began to bark. Lucy sighed. 'SHUT UP MAX,' she called down the stairs. There came a few more barks, followed by silence.

'Thank you,' Lucy muttered, before continuing to go about her going to bed routine.

In the downstairs kitchen, James threw the body of the now dead dog to the tiled floor. His knife was sticking out of Max's stomach. Bending down, he pulled the knife free, wiping the blood off it with a dishtowel that he'd found lying on the kitchen bunker.

Lucy was setting her alarm to get her up at half five in the morning. She heard a thump coming from the bathroom. *Christ*, she thought. *What the hell was Max doing now?*

'MAX,' she shouted. 'GO TO SLEEP.'

She knew full well that it was useless to shout at the dog but still she did it every day. She was about to settle down into her bed, when she heard a sliding noise, followed by another thump.

She felt her temper starting to slip. What the hell was the bloody dog doing?

'MAX, BEHAVE.'

This time she heard a dripping noise. Giving up, Lucy threw the bedspread off her and got up to investigate. She was going to kick Max's ass. He'd had all day to have a carry on and now that she was trying to sleep, he starts.

She left her bedroom and walked over to the bathroom, pushing the door open as far as she could. There was no sign of Max. Where the hell was he? She was sure that the noise had been coming from here.

Lucy was about to turn round and look for Max in another part of the house, when she heard another drip. She headed over to the sink and tightened the taps, but still the dripping continued. She turned around to her bath and pulled the shower curtain open – and froze.

Max hung suspended from the shower nozzle tube, his stomach ripped open and his intestines hanging out. His blood was dripping into the bathtub, staining the white enamel red.

Lucy finally staggered backwards, a scream forming on her lips. Spinning round she was about to make a run for the phone, but instead ran straight into the waiting arms of James.

He brought his fist into Lucy's face sending her reeling. She collapsed to the ground. Moving slightly as she struggled to bring her senses back to what was happening. James frowned slightly. He needed her knocked out. It would make his job easier.

Bending down, he grabbed her by the hair and pulled her head back. He then slammed her head first into the floor. The impact not only knocked her out but it also burst her nose sending a small spray of blood out across the floor.

Walking over her still body, James reached the bathtub and put the plug in. Turning back to Lucy, he bent down and picked her up in his arms. Taking her over to the bathtub, he dropped her down inside of it.

He knelt down beside the bath and reached out to her nightgown, gripping the bottom, he started to tear two strips off it. One strip he forced into her mouth, the other he used to tie her hands together, and attach them to the taps.

Once satisfied that she was secure and not going to be able to struggle against him, should she regain consciousness, he pulled his knife free from its' sheath and placed it down onto the floor.

Reaching back into the bath, James grabbed Lucy's left ankle and pulled it so that the sole of her left foot was flat to the bottom of the bath. This resulted in Lucy's left leg forming a sort of A-shape with her knee being at the top.

Continuing to hold her leg like that with his left hand, he reached down to the floor with his right and picked up the knife. He placed the blade so that point was just below the kneecap bone.

James pushed the blade forward, easily enough through the skin. It met some resistance at the muscle and fat, but he pushed harder and the blade moved through.

The sudden pain brought Lucy back to her senses for a few brief seconds. Her attempts to cry for help were muffled by the nightgown strip that James had forced into her mouth. Seconds later she lapsed back into unconsciousness again. Her blood had begun to ooze out from around the knife and was running down her leg.

James stopped short of pushing the knife right the way through her leg to the other side. Instead he pulled the knife out from the cut he had made and dropped it back to the bathroom floor. With the knife no longer inside of the wound, blood literally began to pour out, pooling around Lucy's limp form.

With his right hand now free, he used it to grab hold of Lucy's left thigh to hold her leg steady when he moved his left hand.

Lifting his left hand up from her ankle, he reached over her injured knee, his fingers resting at the knife wound. After a second, he pushed his fingers into the gash that his knife had made and could feel the warmth of the blood as it poured over his fingers and into the bath.

There was no feeling like this, he thought to himself, pausing for a second. Nothing came close to the thrill of the kill. It didn't matter how many times he did it, it only got better.

Closing his hand into a fist so that he had a grip on the kneecap itself, he wrenched back. The kneecap tore away with a sickening sound, spraying even more blood into the bath and onto the tiled wall.

Pulling himself away from the bath, he stood up to admire his handiwork. Lucy lying in a blood filled bath, her knee completely destroyed and her dog hanging suspended over her, with his intestines hanging out. A rather horrific scene, even if he did say so himself.

Time to finish her off though. He picked the knife up again and used it to sever the strips of gown holding Lucy's hands to the taps. With that done he put the knife back into the sheath, bent down into the bath and scooped Lucy up into his arms, completely uncaring to the fact that he had to place his hands and lower arms into the blood filled bath to get to her.

Turning away from the bath, James carried Lucy from the bathroom. He would finish her off in another room.

TOMRIE RESIDENCE

00:48

Detective John Carter stood in the entrance of Lucy Tomrie's bedroom. Her limp body was lying on her bed. She had been stripped naked and had been cut open from groin to gullet. Her heart had been removed and placed upon her bedside unit for all to see. Her bed sheets were soaked through with blood and her throat had been slashed wide open.

John had never seen such carnage before. The bathroom was literally a blood bath, there was blood trails across the hallway and the state of the body was something that before now he would have said no man was capable of.

Carl Pullman reached the top of the stairs. He had just reached the crime scene and had been directed by the forensics officers below to where John was upstairs. The forensics team weren't happy that either of them were upstairs contaminating the scene, but they had been over ruled, they had insisted however that both of them wore covers over their shoes, latex gloves and that they didn't touch anything.

John turned round to face his boss. 'This is him, isn't it?' he asked, not needing to say the name. With a quick glance into the bedroom Carl just nodded.

'How can a man do this?' John asked Carl.

'I don't know. The only man who even had a clue about James Black was Frank and he's still unconscious since the house fire at the Walker's place. It's just as well that we released that press statement saying that Frank had died otherwise James would probably have finished the job by now.'

'It could still, technically be someone else who did this.'

Carl shook his head. 'No. This is our man. How did we get here anyway? Who called us?'

'There was a 999 call made from this house. No one spoke but the phone was left off the hook, so that we could trace it. The techs found fingerprints on the receiver; they're trying to get a match.'

Carl smirked at this. 'I can save them the bother. The prints belong to James Black. Let me know if anything else turns up.' With that Carl turned and started to leave.

CITY HOSPITAL

TWO DAYS LATER

12:12

Catherine Thorn was sitting beside her comatose husband, holding his hand. She had been here every day since he had been admitted more than a month earlier. The doctors said that they had no idea when Frank would waken up, if at all.

Catherine believed that he would wake up, he had to. The doctors had said that he probably wouldn't survive the ride into the hospital after his fall from the window of the Walker house, but he had. He was a fighter, always had been and she believed he always would be once he was well again that was.

Her own doctor had signed her off work with stress, so that she could come to sit by her husband every day, and every day she was here hoping and praying that there would be some change in her husband's condition.

She had only been married to Frank for two years but had known him for longer. She had seen his initial investigation into the murders from 1998, and she was aware of how it had affected him then. His reaction a month ago, when he realised that the killer was not only alive but after revenge, had been extreme to day the least.

Just then his hand twitched. Catherine started, unsure whether she had imagined it or not. She reached out to take hold of his hand, hoping as she did so that it wasn't her imagination.

Seconds later, she was rewarded with another twitch, and then finally Frank's fingers tightened slightly over her own.

'Frank,' Catherine whispered, hardly daring to believe. His eyes began to flutter open and he tried to focus on the room.

He tried to whisper her name but his throat was too dry.

'Frank,' Catherine whispered again, tears of joy starting to roll down her cheeks.

LOTHIAN AND BORDERS POLICE STATION

14:00

Carl sat slumped over his desk. He had the original case files from the 1998 police investigation spread out all over his desk. The autopsy reports, police reports, forensic evidence lists and photographs of all of the victims. He had details of how James had killed Sally Nicholson, the Walkers and now Lucy Tomrie.

He'd had these files for weeks and had poured over them like a man obsessed. He was trying to find a pattern but the only pattern in the files was the level of violence that this man administered to his victims both physically and mentally.

Deep down he knew that it was a waste of time, but he had to try something. He couldn't just sit around waiting for James to strike again.

The forensics team had confirmed that the fingerprints on the phone in Lucy Tomrie's house were indeed that of James Black.

Just then his office phone started ringing, tearing him away from his thoughts. He reached out and answered it.

'Yes,' he said impatiently.

'Hi, it's Catherine Thorn,' came the reply. 'I thought you'd like to know that Frank is awake. He's still very weak but he is awake.'

'That's great news,' Carl replied, a glimmer of hope appearing. 'Is there any chance that he would be up to a quick visit? I could really do with his advice.'

'I don't think that would be a good idea,' Catherine said.

'I would only be a few minutes, honestly. It might be the difference between catching this killer and someone else being killed.'

There was a moment's silence on the other end of the phone. Finally Catherine spoke up again. 'Alright but if he doesn't want anything to do with this, your not to press him. Is that a deal?'

'Absolutely,' Carl replied.

With that decided, the two of them hung up and Carl got ready to head over to the hospital.

CITY HOSPITAL

14:56

Frank smiled weakly as Carl entered the room. He was in a sitting position with the back of the hospital bed raised to support him. Catherine stood by his side, still not very happy about the discussion that was about to take place.

'Frank,' Carl called to him. 'Feeling better?'

'A little,' Frank replied. 'But that's not why you're here, is it?'

'Yes and no,' Carl said. 'Of course, I'm glad that you are feeling better, but unfortunately, events are rather pressing and I need your help.'

'James is still alive. Isn't he?'

Carl nodded his agreement.

'Why hasn't he come for me? To finish what he started?'

'We told the press that you had died in hospital and even staged a fake funeral for you. James believes that you're dead.'

'Ah. Now you want me to help you to catch him. Is that right?'

'He's already killed since the fight you had with him and we think that it is only a matter of time before he strikes again. We have no idea what to do to try and capture him. You are the only one who ever came close.'

'You're not going to stumble across a pattern or find him by chance. He's too good at what he does. You can, however, make him come to you. There is no guarantee though, that it wont backfire and more people will die, maybe you.'

'It's a risk that I'll have to take. How do I make him come to me?'

'I was never able to work out much about him, but one thing that I do know is that he likes a challenge. Hold a press conference. Challenge him to come out and after you, instead of innocent people. I think you'll find that all of a sudden you become popular.'

Carl was about to ask more questions but Frank held his hand up. 'Enough,' he said. 'I'm tired. I need to rest. If I think of anything else I'll let you know.'

Carl nodded reluctantly, remembering his agreement with Catherine not to press after Frank had made it clear that enough was enough. He thanked them both and left them alone, mulling over what Frank had said.

NEXT DAY

09:33

James sat at the wheel of the latest car that he had stolen. That morning's newspaper was in front of him. He usually followed the news stories about himself, to see what was being said. How much was being made up and how far from the front page his stories were.

Today he was both surprised and slightly pissed off at the news stories about him. It would appear that the police were not only suggesting that he was a coward, but they were openly challenging him to a confrontation. This was slightly unexpected and he reread the article again to get the name of the man issuing the challenge. Carl Pullman.

Okay Carl, he thought. If you want to face me, then so be it but it would be on his terms and by his rules. Slowly, a plan began to hatch in his mind. He would need to get some stuff and as such it would take a few days before he would be ready.

THAT NIGHT

01:10

The man twisted and turned in his restless sleep. In his dreams he was butchering people. The faces of the people were a blur but that wasn't important, it was the fact that he was killing them and was enjoying it.

All of a sudden the man woke up with a start, sweat lashing off of him. The images of the dream still fresh in his mind. He'd been having these types of dreams now for the last three nights and what bothered him the most was that instead of disgusting him, they actually excited him, to the extent that he was aroused by them.

He was putting the dreams down to the stress that he was feeling at work. Maybe he should take a holiday.

Knowing that he wouldn't be able to get back to sleep that night, he got up and headed to the kitchen to get himself a drink of water and clear his head.

LOTHIAN AND BORDERS POLICE STATION

TWO DAYS LATER

11:02

Carl was once again poring over the files that the police had on James Black. He was disappointed that James hadn't risen to the bait over the newspaper articles that had been published two days earlier. He was now thinking of having another press conference saying that as thought James was a coward and his failure to meet the challenge proved it. He didn't really think that it would work however. He would have to think of another way to capture the madman.

BRITTANIC PRIMARY SCHOOL

14:20

James strode into the building, a gun held in his right hand and a rucksack slung over his left shoulder. His knife was in its sheath on his belt. It was time to accept Carl's challenge.

The corridors were deserted, just as James had planned for it to happen. Classes were still in progress at the moment. He made his way down the corridor to where the assembly hall was. He knew the layout of the school as he had scoped it out yesterday. Schools really should have much better security, after all here he was in the middle of one, with murder on his mind and no one was challenging him. After all of the instances in recent years with people just walking into schools and killing innocent children, you would think that the local councils would learn. Still, it made what he wanted to do easier and maybe they would tighten security after what he had in mind.

He reached the assembly hall and kicked the door open. Inside the hall was a class of about twenty young children and one primary teacher. The children were all sitting in chairs facing the front, but they had all turned round towards him upon hearing his dramatic entrance.

'NO ONE MOVE,' James ordered, raising the gun to make his point.

'You,' he said to the teacher. 'Do you have the key for this room?'

The teacher nodded, afraid to try and lie to him in case he hurt either her or more importantly, the children.

'Give it to me,' James ordered.

The teacher moved slowly across the hall, reaching into her pocket to give him the key.

'Well done,' James muttered when he had the key. 'Back over there with the kids.'

The teacher turned to go, but hesitated. 'I don't know what you want but please just let the children go,' she tried reasoning with him.

'Get back over there, NOW,' James ordered. 'Or you all die.'

The teacher started moving back to her wards. Her name was Susie Goodman. She didn't know what this man wanted or what he had in mind but she was damned if she was going to let him hurt the kids. She had to do something

Turning to the door, James locked it so that there was no way out. He placed the rucksack on the ground and reaching into his trouser pocket, pulled out a mobile phone, which he used to phone the hotline for people who had sighted him.

Once he was put through to Carl Pullman's extension, he was put on hold for a few seconds. Finally it was answered.

'Hello,' came Carl's less than enthusiastic voice.

'Carl Pullman?' James inquired.

'Yes. Who's this?'

'I believe that you want me to accept a challenge to face you.'

'James Black?' Carl replied. 'I have several nutters a day calling me claiming that they're James Black. You're going to need to prove you are who you say you are.'

'Listen to me,' James cut him off. 'I don't have the patience for this, so I'm going to cut to the chase. I'm holding a primary school class and their teacher hostage. You have only twenty minutes to get here before I start to kill them off. You can bring as many of your officers as you want, but only you are to come inside of the building. Also alert the press. I want them to see your challenge backfiring and your death. To show that I am serious about being who I say I am and what I'm threatening, I shall execute a hostage now.'

Without saying anything else, James raised the gun and fired one shot. It hit Susie Goodman square in the forehead, killing her instantly and ending any hopes she had of trying to save the kids from this madman. The kids begun screaming, but were quickly silenced when James pointed the gun at them and ordered them to shut up.

'The children no longer have a teacher,' James said into the phone. 'I suggest that you don't be late as I will kill one child for every minute that you are.'

'You sick son of a bitch,' Carl hissed into the phone. 'The challenge was to face me, not kill children.'

James smiled at himself. 'Times a wasting,' he said. 'I'm at the Brittanic Primary School. When you get here; phone me on this number.'

He began to reel off the number of the mobile phone. After today he would have to ditch the phone but that didn't matter.

'Oh and it might be an idea to evacuate the rest of the building.'

He hung up the phone and turned his attention to the rucksack on the ground. The sound of the children's whimpering and crying was starting to get on his nerves. Training the gun on any of the children who might move, he opened the rucksack with his other hand, to reveal a crude but effective hand made explosive device with a timer attached to its side.

Looking down at his watch, he decided that Carl still had eighteen minutes to get here. With that in mind, he set the timer for forty-five minutes and started the count down.

TWENTY ONE MINUTES LATER

Carl pulled up at the top of the drive, reaching for his mobile phone as he did so. He had pre-programmed the number that James had given him into his phone so that he could speed dial him when he got here. Uniformed police officers were also arriving and were about to start evacuating the other children and teachers. The media was on route as well, just like James had instructed.

Hitting the 'call' button on his phone, he put it to his ear. It was answered on the other end on the first ring.

'Three minutes late Carl. Three children down.'

'You didn't have to kill anyone for the sake of three minutes. You knew that I was coming.'

'And you knew that I was serious,' James countered. 'Enough chat. I want you to make your way to the assembly hall. Only you will be allowed to enter. If you bring anyone else to the hall, I will kill every last one of these children. Leave your gun and bring a pair of handcuffs.'

'And what if I say no?' Carl asked.

'Then the media will see that you failed to live up to your own challenge and they will also see that the police were powerless to stop a serial killer adding a whole class of children to his victim list. Remember it was your lot who forced my hand to do this. You asked me to come out of hiding and face you head on. I'm giving you that chance now.

'If you're not here in the next five minutes then I will assume that you have chickened out and I'll kill the lot of the children.'

FOUR MINUTES LATER

Carl knocked on the door of the assembly and seconds later heard the sound of a key in the lock. The door opened to reveal a small blond haired girl. At back of the room, James stood with his gun trained on her.

'Are you alone?' he shouted at Carl.

'Yes.'

'Good. Come in. Sit down over there,' he said pointing to a chair at the far end of the room.

Carl did as he was instructed. As he sat down he saw the bodies of the three children and their teacher. He'd hoped that James had been bluffing when he had said that he had killed these people but he should have known better.

He watched as James moved back to the entrance of the hall, taking the keys back off the blond girl. James bent down to the blond girl.

'What's your name?' he asked.

'Samantha,' the scared reply came, her voice trembling in fear.

'Well Samantha, can you go and sit with that man over there please,' he said pointing at Carl. She nodded and started to make her way over towards him.

Standing at the entrance of the hall, with the gun pointing at Carl, James opened the door.

'The rest of you can go,' he said. Without any hesitation, the rest of the children broke for the door, screaming as they did so. When the last of them was gone James closed and locked the door, placing the keys into his pocket.

James glanced at the timer of the bomb, which Carl was still unaware of. He was setting this up so that Carl would be killed in the blast and it would be something that the press would lap up.

18:56

18:55

18:54

Moving over to where Carl and Samantha were sitting, James trained the gun on Carl.

'Bet you regret your press conference now,' James smirked. 'Did you bring your handcuffs?'

'Yes,' Carl replied.

'Good. Place one cuff on your right wrist and place both hands behind the chair. Time is short.'

'What do you mean, 'time is short'?'

'Just that,' James replied.

'Why can't you let the girl go?' Carl asked.

'Back up plan,' came the reply. 'A hostage in case something goes wrong. Now do what you're told.'

Reluctantly, Carl cuffed his right hand and placed both hands behind the back of the chair. James moved round to the back of the chair and knelt down so that he could cuff Carl's hands together.

17:46

17:45

17:44

Waiting until he could feel James grab a hold of his hands, Carl leaned forward slightly and then pushed himself backwards. The chair toppled back into the crouching James, knocking him to the ground under the weight.

Carl twisted round and pulled his hands free. The handcuffs were dangling freely from his right wrist. Already James was pushing the chair off of him and getting back to his feet.

Carl knew that he had to press his advantage now or he would never get another chance. Turning to face James, he lashed out with his fist, which connected with the killer's nose, bursting it.

In the corner of the room, Samantha cowered. Tears running down her face, her fear rooting her to the spot.

Meanwhile Carl continued to push forward with his assault, not giving James a chance to come back with an attack of his own.

James raised the gun with the intention of finishing it once and for all but Carl threw himself at him. The two men fell to the ground. The jolt of the impact caused James to pull the trigger of the gun accidentally.

The sound of the gun going off echoed across the hall, sounding impossibly loud. Across in the corner of the room, Samantha slumped forward, having caught the bullet in her chest.

James was first to his feet. Throwing the gun to the ground, he pulled the knife from its sheath and swung it at Carl who was still getting up. The blade cut through his shirtsleeve and into his arm.

Crying out, Carl twisted backwards away from the knife. This time it was James who was on the attack. He lunged forwards at Carl, forcing him further backwards and slowly into a corner.

With his back getting closer and closer to the wall, Carl decided to fight back again. He waited until James took another swipe at him with his knife and with lightening reflexes grabbed hold of James's wrist, stopping the attack. With his other hand he threw a punch, which landed square in his opponent's face.

James staggered backwards, the knife falling from his hand to the ground.

13:01

13:00

12:59

Carl saw the gun lying on the ground and made a scramble for it. He had to finish this off and get Samantha to a hospital. As it was she was lying in an expanding pool of her own blood and he didn't even know whether she was still alive.

He reached the gun and was about to pick it up when he noticed the bomb sitting in the corner of the room. Now he knew what James had meant when he had said that time was short.

By this time, James had picked his knife back up again and was marching towards Carl. He too was aware that time was pressing.

Carl heard the footsteps of James as he closed the distance between them and he grabbed the gun from the floor and spun round to face the threat.

'RIGHT THERE,' he shouted at James. He expected even James to stop when he had a gun pointed at him but he continued on towards him regardless.

With not enough time to issue another warning, Carl aimed and squeezed the trigger. The gun clicked empty and before Carl could think about his next action, James grabbed him and pushed him against the wall.

'Do you really think that I would be stupid enough to throw a loaded gun away? If you'd bothered to look properly at the bodies of the teacher and her three brats, then you'd have seen that I used more bullets than I needed to kill them. Let's just say that I was also killing time. When you came in I only had one bullet left.'

10:10

10:09

Carl brought his knee up into his James's groin. The effect being that the killer doubled over in pain, his grip on Carl gone. Carl followed through with a heavy punch to the face, knocking James down to the ground.

Running past James, Carl reached Samantha. He turned her over to check whether, she was still alive. She was, barely. Picking her up in his arms he made his way to the entrance of the hall. Reaching the doors, he remembered that James had locked the door and that he had the keys in his pocket. He needed to get those keys and now.

Before he could do anything else however, he felt a searing pain. Behind him James had plunged his knife into Carl's back. Unable to help himself at the sudden pain, Carl dropped Samantha. Her body hit the ground with a thud although she was past the point of being conscious and didn't feel the impact.

Grabbing the knife, James hauled it out of the wound and spun Carl round to face him. Stabbing him in the stomach and then pushing him down the ground. Carl tried to get back to his feet but slipped on his own blood.

09:23

09:22

09:21

'How heroic,' James commented sarcastically. 'Still trying to save the lives of others even though it reduces the chance of your own escape. I'll save you the bother of having to worry about young Samantha here.'

With that James reached down and pulled the unconscious girl up. Raising his knife above her head, he brought it down hard. The steel blade shattered her skull and burst into her brain killing her instantly.

Carl was pulling himself onto his feet, trying to ignore the pain as best as he could. His shirt was soaked through with blood on both sides. Grasping one of the chairs in his hands he picked it up and swung it at James.

James looked up from his attack on Samantha, too late. The chair hit him full force in the face, knocking him down to the ground. Carl raised it up again and smashed it down hard onto his fallen opponent.

07:41

07:40

07:39

James lay on the ground unconscious from the two blows from the chair. Carl was starting to feel incredibly light headed from the blood loss but he never the less continued to fight to stay upright.

He reached down and turned James over, padding down each trouser pocket for the keys to the assembly hall. Having found them he reached inside to pull them out. James started to stir slightly.

07:00

06:59

06:58

With the keys now in his hand, Carl staggered over to the door. Harder and harder to keep his balance, his vision starting to show black spots. He reached the door and started trying to find the right key for the lock. With the second attempt he got the right one. Twisting the key he pushed the door open and stumbled out.

The corridor was deserted. It would appear that the evacuation had been finished. Good.

05:45

05:44

05:43

Carl reached the entrance to the school and almost fell down a small set of stairs that led to the entrance. The police officers that had been evacuating the pupils started forward to help him. The media were also there, filming and taking pictures of him as he struggled down the stairs. Detective John Carter had arrived by this point as well and he rushed forward to help his boss.

'Get everyone further back,' Carl mumbled. 'There's a bomb inside. It will go of in a few minutes.'

'What?' John asked unable to comprehend what he was being told.

'Just do it,' Carl ordered.

Without any further questions, John ordered that the police officers move everyone further back straight away.

Inside of the assembly hall, James started to come to. His head was thumping. He suddenly remembered where he was and scrambled to his feet, angry for allowing himself to be beaten like that, and for allowing his carefully constructed plan to go horribly wrong.

Never mind, he had to get out of here now before the bomb went off. He glanced at the bomb as he was leaving the room.

00:29

00:28

00:27

'Shit,' he muttered. He started to jog out of the hall and down the hallway.

00:10

00:09

00:08

He reached the entrance in time to throw himself down the set of stairs and scramble back to his feet. He could see the police and the media at the entrance. He could also see what he assumed was Carl receiving medical attention from the medics that the police had called for the released children.

00:02

00:01

00:00

The explosion ripped through the assembly hall and part of the outer wall. The shock wave shattering windows and knocking James back off his feet. Fiery debris started to fall down around him.

One piece of brickwork hit his head as he was trying to get back to his feet. Coupled with the blows he had received from the chair earlier, this was enough to knock him out again.

A minute later, satisfied that the worst of the damage that the bomb was going to do had already been done, John started jogging forward towards the fallen killer. He had three police officers behind him.

In the school, the automatic fire alarms were ringing and smoke was billowing out from the destroyed assembly hall.

John reached James and pinned him down to the ground in case he came to. One of the other officers cuffed James's hands behind his back. Finally, John thought. They had James Black.

'Stick him in the back of a police car. When he wakes up, read him his rights,' John ordered the three officers. 'And under no circumstances, underestimate him.'

John headed back to where Carl was, who was about to get into the back of an ambulance.

'Tell me, we got him,' he said.

'We got him,' John confirmed.

PART 3

EDINBURGH

ONE YEAR LATER

21:00

The man stood across the road from the late night chemist store. He was standing at a bus stop so that it didn't look suspicious whilst he was watching. He saw the shop clerk in the chemists move towards the glass door and lock it. She turned the OPEN sign around so that it read CLOSED and started to head back towards the heart of the shop.

Inside of the chemist shop, Mary went behind the counter and turned on the small portable radio that she brought in when she was working late. The music started to blare out through the empty store. She only had half an hour to go before she finished work for the night. In that time she had to secure the cash and drugs, tidy up the shelves slightly and get the shop ready for the next day when the manager started work.

Outside the man left the bus stop and started to head towards the chemists. He was dressed in black and was wearing a long black raincoat with black leather gloves. In his right hand he was carrying a green plastic carrier bag. Inside of which, he had several things that he would need for what he planned to do to the shop clerk, whose name he didn't even know.

He continued to walk on past the shop and followed the street round until he came to a street running parallel to the one that the chemists store was in. The back entrance of the chemist shop was facing this new street. It was where the deliveries were dropped off and transported into building, although there were none at the moment.

He reached for the door handle to try his luck. It was locked, still it wouldn't take him long to get in. He knew how to pick locks, even the most difficult of them. He started to work on the lock.

He knew what he was planning to do to the shop clerk, and even though the small part of him that was still remotely sane was telling him not to do it, he was going to anyway. This wouldn't be the first time he had killed in cold blood but it was still a relatively new thing to him. A year ago he had started having the dreams of murder and death, and they had excited him more than anything else until finally three months ago he had finally caved in to the desires and committed his first murder. He had decided to base himself on Edinburgh's most famous serial killer, James Black, who had in turn been caught just weeks after the dreams had begun and had been sentenced to life imprisonment the same week that he had committed his first murder.

The lock clicked and the man turned the handle to open the door and let himself in. He could hear the sound of the music from the radio, which he had seen the clerk turn on after she had locked the door. Moving silently through the back storeroom, he entered the back of the shop. He could see Mary in the main shop floor tidying the customer area.

The man placed the plastic bag down at his feet and started to move forward. He was at the back of the shop where the prescriptions were made up. Drugs of all sorts surrounded him. He moved down a single step that took him behind the glass service counter where the non-prescription drugs were being kept.

All it would have taken was for Mary to turn round from her tidying and she would have seen the man. He was in plain sight, but she was quite happy listening to her blaring music and pulling the stock forward on the shelves so that they looked fuller than they were.

With the music covering the sound of his footsteps, the man stepped out from behind the counter onto the customer floor area. Only a metre or so away from her now. He could feel the adrenaline as the kill neared and like the previous times that he had done this, he could feel himself getting aroused. Was this what James Black had felt? If so he could now finally understand why he did what he did.

The radio started playing a song that Mary didn't really like that much.

'Not a chance,' she muttered to herself, turning round with the intention of changing stations.

She didn't even have time to scream when she saw the man. He brought his fist into her face, sending her backwards into a sunglasses stand, which fell over under the impact.

Mary fell to the floor, her lower lip and gum burst from the punch, the blood tasting coppery in her mouth. The man advanced on her. This time she did have time to cry out for help.

'SOMEONE HELP. PLEASE HELP ME,' she called out but there was no one to hear her calls and no one in the street to see the violence through the glass door.

'Shut up,' the man ordered in a calm collected voice, as he leaned down and punched Mary again in the face, this time bursting her nose. He then grabbed her hair and started to pull upwards.

'On your feet,' he demanded. Despite her fear, Mary got to her feet. Tears were running down her face and mixing with the blood that was running out of her burst nose.

'Please don't kill me,' she gasped through her tears.

The man looked at her and saw the pain and fear in her eyes. She had done nothing to him. What was he doing? His resolve began to buckle and the part of him that was still sane began to try and take control. What had he become over the last few months?

He felt his eyes well up slightly at these thoughts and a single tear ran down his face. Mary saw this and pressed onwards, desperate to try and get out of this alive.

'Please. I won't tell anyone. Just let me go.'

The man turned away from Mary, still holding his grip in her hair. He blinked to try and clear his vision slightly. The sane side of him was falling back into the shadows of his mind and the side that had become overexposed to the type of violence that he was about to commit took over again.

Without turning back to face her he started to move forward back the way that he had come in, pulling Mary with him by the hair.

'No, please,' Mary begged, knowing that somehow she had almost gotten out and that now she was back to square one again.

The man dragged her to the service counter and pushed her against it, moving himself so that he was behind her and up against her, his hand still in her hair. Mary could feel the man pressed hard up against her backside and she could tell that he was savouring it, but there was nothing that she could do. Wedged between her attacker and the glass counter, coupled with the man's grip in her hair, she couldn't even turn round let alone put up a fight.

For a few seconds, the man continued to be torn between doing this and letting her go. Then finally he made his final decision. Pulling her head as far back as it would go, he shoved it forward as hard as he could. She had time for a quick scream before her face connected with the glass unit and the surface shattered under the impact. Shards of glass were cutting and gouging into her skin. Blood began to rain down onto the flu drugs below, creating a strange effect with the broken glass.

Pulling her head back out of the counter, the man hauled her back to her feet. The incident with the unit had had the desired effect. Mary was now unconscious from the pain and or the fear. The man didn't care which.

He dragged her limp body behind the counter to the prescription area, where the unit would hide what he was about to do, should anyone pass the shop and look in the door window.

Clearing the floor of obstacles, he laid Mary on her back. He pushed both her feet together and pulled her arms out at a right angle from her body, so that she was lying in the shape of the cross.

The man got back up and walked over to where he had left his plastic bag. Picking it up, he brought it over and opened it up. Inside were several large roofing nails and a solid looking hammer.

The man placed one of the roofing nails over Mary's upturned palm and raised the hammer to do what he had set out to do.

NEXT DAY

8:45

Detective John Carter arrived at the crime scene at the chemist shop and almost about turned when he saw what had happened to the poor woman the night before. There were patches of blood everywhere. The main customer area was a mess and the counter was smashed with blood patches on the goods below.

What was worst about this though was when he got to the back of the shop and saw the literally crucified body of who had been identified as Mary Patterson. Roofing nails had been hammered through her hands into the floor. Around each wound the blood had spread and congealed. Her face was covered in cuts and had pieces of glass sticking out of it. Her throat had been slashed open in what John could only hope had happened before the crucifixion as the thought of anyone having to live through that made his stomach turn.

He turned back to the main area of the shop. He could see the manager outside being spoken to by the police. He was very pale looking and in a state of shock. After all, he had found Mary's body when he had come to open up.

'John,' he heard the voice behind him. John turned round to face the person addressing him. It was his boss, Carl Pullman.

'What do you think?' Carl asked.

John sighed surprised. 'It's definitely our man. Do we have any clues?'

'Not really,' Carl answered, shaking his head slightly. 'Still no fingerprints. We might have hair and fibre but we have to wait for the boys from forensics to get back to us. The bottom line is that any clues we do find could have come from anyone. The manager, the responding officers and a few others who shouldn't really have been here until the forensics team had gotten here first. In fact the only reason we're being allowed here is because there has been so much crime scene contamination already and they've already gone.'

'What about that CCTV camera?' John asked pointing at a camera in the corner of the room. 'Does the tape show anything?'

'We can't find the tape. The killer must have taken it before he left.'

'So we have four murders over the last few months and still no clues. At least in that respect he's as good as James Black was.'

Carl smirked at this. 'Yeah. Here we go again.'

'Are we any closer to getting a profile together on the killer?' John asked.

Once again, Carl shook his head. 'No, not really. The only thing they seem to say is that each murder is becoming sloppier than the last. That he is getting too cocky. Although if he is too sloppy then how come we can't find any clues.'

'Do these profilers actually read the case files?'

'Apparently,' Carl answered.

'What about Frank Thorn?' John asked.

Carl's eyes narrowed slightly. 'What about him?'

'Have you tried asking him for help. He came closer to getting into James Black's head than anyone else did. Maybe he could help us now.'

'Frank is out. He doesn't work for us anymore.'

‘I know that. But maybe we could ask him for his help anyway. Bring him back out of his retirement for one last case. Purely as an adviser.’

Carl thought about it for a few seconds. ‘All right. It’s worth a try, but I’ll go to speak to him. You continue to follow any other leads.’

‘What leads?’ John asked. ‘There isn’t any. Not really.’

‘Just do it,’ Carl ordered before turning round to leave the scene.

THORN RESIDENCE

12TH FLOOR OF TOWERBLOCK FLATS

SIGHTHILL

EDINBURGH

9:31

Frank opened the front door, a frown already on his face as he had seen who it was through the spy hole.

‘Carl,’ he greeted casually. ‘Come in.’

He led him through to the small living room that he had. His wife Catherine was reading a book in one of the chairs.

‘Hi Catherine,’ Carl greeted. ‘How you’re doing?’

‘Carl,’ she greeted suspiciously. She knew that this wasn’t a social call. He had only visited once since Frank had been released from hospital. There had been some concern that during the trial, James would learn that Frank was alive, but James surprised everyone by pleading guilty to all the charges of murder and assault. With that plea there was no trial and Frank was never called upon to give evidence. To this day James still believed that Frank was dead.

‘Catherine. Could you excuse us please?’ Frank asked his wife. ‘I don’t imagine that this will take long. Will it Carl?’

‘Probably not,’ Carl replied.

Catherine stood up and left to head into the kitchen to make some coffee. She pushed the door closed as she did so, to give them some privacy.

‘Sit down,’ Frank said to Carl. Once they were both seated, Frank spoke again. ‘Ok what is it that you want, Carl? We both know that this is not a social call.’

Carl pulled out a file that he had been holding under his arm and handed it to Frank. Frank accepted the file, opened it and started to flick through the contents. They were copies of the police files on the killer that had struck the previous night, although the most recent murder was still incomplete in the file.

‘Very nice,’ Frank said as he handed them back to Carl. ‘What do you expect me to do with them?’

‘Well I was hoping for your help.’

‘I’m retired from all that now, Carl. I will not be dragged into it again. It almost cost me my life when I went after the last killer.’

‘Oh right. So James is locked up and you’re happy? You can just ignore the rest of the sick people out there?’

‘Pretty much,’ Frank answered. ‘I can sleep well at night, knowing that James Black is locked up and that my wife and I are safe. I will not do anything that will risk that.’

‘What if we’d never caught James? Would you still have retired?’

‘No,’ Frank replied. ‘James would have kept coming for me as soon as he found out that I was still alive. I would have been forced to stay in the job to try and stop him.’

‘What if this copy cat killer comes to try and finish off what James didn’t?’

‘Just because he’s copying James, doesn’t mean that he is continuing where James left off. Besides don’t you think that he would have shown face by now and it’s not common knowledge that I’m alive?

‘You won’t even take a look at the files then?’

Frank shook his head. ‘Sorry Carl. I wish you the best of luck but there is nothing I can do.’

‘Innocent people will die you know?’

‘Emotional blackmail will not get you anywhere, Carl.’

Carl stood back up in exasperation. ‘I’m sorry to have wasted your time, Frank. I’ll be off. I can see myself out.’

With that Carl turned and left the room, heading back to the front door. He hadn’t really expected Frank to help, but he had to try. Leaving the flat he headed to the lifts to take him back downstairs to where he had parked his car.

Back in the flat, Frank sat pondering over what Carl had said. He could probably have helped but that would have run the risk of backfiring like the Black case had all those years ago. If he had known the costs of accepting that case back in 1998 then he would have never have taken it. No, he decided. He was making the right decision.

MAXIMUM SECURITY PRISON

EDINBURGH

10:58

Detective John Carter was waiting in the visitor room. There was bullet-proof glass separating his side of the table with the other side. The other side was still empty but John had pulled strings to get a talk with James Black.

Carl had told him to follow other leads and since the killer seemed to be basing himself on James black’s aimless M.O. then talking to James seemed like a good idea. Besides what else was there for him to do? There was very little evidence for him to use or follow up on.

On the other side of the glass, the only door opened and two armed guards entered, with James Black in between them. He was dressed in navy blue overalls and both his hands were cuffed in front of him.

He was escorted to a chair that sat directly in front of the window and directly in front of John on the other side of the glass.

John reached up to pick up the phone on his side of the glass and James did the same on his end. The only difference being that James had to raise both hands, as the cuffs wouldn't allow for anything else.

'Why are you here?' James asked.

'I need your help,' John replied.

James smiled at this. 'You need my help. You must be desperate. Why should I help you anyway?'

'Someone has begun murdering people using your old M.O. an…'

'And you're screwed for trying to catch him again,' James interrupted.

'Is that right?'

'Yes,' John said grudgingly.

'Still doesn't explain why I should help you though, does it? I mean what's in it for me?'

'You get to do something decent for once. Prove to the world that you've still got a part of you that's human.'

James outright grinned at this. 'Why would I either want to or care what the world thinks of me. I do what I do and what the world thinks is irrelevant.'

'But that's not entirely true now. Is it? I mean you went to a lot of bother to become front page headlines and the only reason you were caught is because of that challenge in the paper that Carl Pullman made to you.'

James's grin disappeared at this. 'Ok,' he said. 'I'll rephrase that statement. I do care slightly what the world thinks about me, but I sure as hell don't want to be remembered as a nice guy.'

'Ok,' John said. He was going to have to try another tactic. 'Do you really want a killer that you spawned getting the press headlines? Surely if it isn't you, it shouldn't be anyone. How long before the press start to say that this new killer is better than you because he hasn't been caught?'

James paused for a minute, before grinning again. 'Nice try. That's not going to work. Keep bringing them on though. You're killing time for me.'

'Ok, James. What would it take for you to help us?'

James thought about it then leaned forward as he said his request.

'You're right. I can help and I do have price. I want to see the four crime scenes.'

'No problem,' John said. 'I can have the files copied and brought in to you.'

'No you misunderstand me,' James said. 'I said that I want to see the crime scenes. I meant in person. The chance to stand in the chaos one last time is what I want.'

'No,' John said. 'That's not going to happen. Even if I trusted you, which I don't, I don't have that kind of sway or authority.'

'I'm sure that when you get desperate enough, you'll find a way,' James retorted. 'Until then, you know where you can find me.'

With that James stood up and the two guards appeared at either side of him. 'I'm ready to go back now,' James told them.

Seconds later, James was gone from the room, leaving John with his thoughts.

12:12

John sat in his car thinking over what James had said. He was right, John probably could arrange for a 24-hour day release with an armed escort but he would have to call in nearly every favour owed him to do so. If something went wrong it would be John that got in serious trouble though, not James. He decided to leave it for now and see if Carl had had any luck trying to speak to Frank.

GRAY RESIDENCE

EIGHT DAYS LATER

23:23

Brian Gray helped his pregnant wife, Sarah into the bath. They had been married for a little under two years and were expecting their first child in about a month and a half. He eased her down into the bathtub, before standing back up again.

'Let me know when you're ready to get out again,' he told his wife. She could probably do it all herself but he was paranoid about any unnecessary strains to her health and she had long since stopped telling him that she could manage fine without his help.

'Will do,' she replied. 'Can you close the door on your way out?'

'Ok,' he said as he pulled the door closed and left.

Outside in their back garden, the man sat on the patio wrestling with his demons. The urge to kill again was becoming stronger with each passing day since his last victim. It seemed to be that yes, killing removed the urge for a while but it always came back. Now it was taking less and less time after each murder. His remaining sane side wanted to stop and knew that the only way for him to stop was to be caught, as the man would never ignore the urge for any length of time. It was too strong.

The man hated and loved what he had become at the same time and it was tearing him apart. Abruptly he stood bolt upright. He knew what he was going to do. He was dressed and prepared for what he knew he was about to do. Again he wore all black and his long black raincoat with leather gloves. This time he didn't have a plastic bag with him. All he had was a large kitchen knife in his coat pocket. That was all he would need for tonight.

He had no idea who was in the house or whose garden he was sitting in. He had randomly chosen it, hadn't done any research for it or anything. He wanted to satisfy his urge to kill right now.

Back inside of the house Sarah was out of the bath and in her nightgown, only minutes away from heading off to bed for the night. It was late after all. Brian was about to go back downstairs to watch the football highlights on T.V. He was just making sure that she had everything that she needed.

'Are you sure you've done everything?' he asked.

'Brian,' she came back at him. 'I'm a big girl now. I know how to go to bed. Away and watch your football. Ok.'

'Ok,' he said. 'Sorry, I don't mean to smother you as much as that.'

'I know,' she replied. 'I'm not angry. I'm just saying that I can get into bed without your help.'

Brian nodded his understanding before kissing his wife goodnight and heading down the stairs, to watch his football. Sarah meanwhile climbed into her bed and pulled the blankets over her. The sooner this baby was born the better. Not long to go now, as she was more than seven months pregnant.

Outside the man had once again used his knowledge to unlock the back door of the house and let himself in. He was now slinking in the shadows of the kitchen. He could see the stairs from here and could see Brian coming back down them and entering what the man could only assume was the living room.

The man realised that he had no idea how many people were in the house at the moment and that maybe this wasn't a good idea after all. Pausing for a few minutes he finally decided to carry on anyway. His urge must be satisfied.

He slid out of the kitchen, keeping his eyes open for anyone else in the house. No one was about. Turning to look into the living room he saw Brian sitting in front of the T.V. watching football, listening to the sound through headphones. It couldn't have made the man's job easier if he had tried. The headphones did suggest that there was someone up the stairs, probably in their bed trying to get to sleep. No matter, he would take care of this one first.

Pulling the knife out of his coat pocket, the man advanced on Brian from behind. Reaching him, he reached and clamped his left hand over Brian's mouth to stifle the cries for help. Brian started but it was too late. He started to struggle against his attacker but the man was too strong.

Upstairs, Sarah heard a thump followed by the sound of something breaking. What the hell was going on downstairs? She sat up in the bed as best as she could.

'Brian,' she called out. 'Brian. What are you doing?'

When she didn't get an answer she threw the blankets off her and started to struggle out of the bed to her feet. Christ, she thought. He's probably wearing those damn earphones again.

The man was heading up the stairs now. He had finished checking the other rooms downstairs for anyone else in the house and now he was heading in the direction of the voice that he had heard.

Sarah reached her bedroom door and opened it, freezing when she was confronted by this stranger in her house. Before she could scream, the man had grabbed her by the throat and was pushing her back into the room. The knife in his right hand was glistening red with Brian's blood.

Sarah tried to hit out at the man with her fists, but he kept her at arms length, before throwing her across the room into a wooden wardrobe at the side of the room. She hit the wardrobe door front on and slid down against it. Pain searing through her abdomen, she immediately feared for her unborn babies life. Tears of pain and fear running down her cheeks, Sarah started to try and get herself back to her feet but her condition was making it too hard for her to get back to her feet.

The man paused again, looking down at her. No, part of him cried out. She's pregnant. The man advanced slowly. Hearing the voice of humanity inside of him but ignoring it all the same. The thought of killing this pregnant woman was actually turning him on slightly and he could feel himself getting psychically aroused.

He paused again as the sane side of him again tried to regain control, which was happening less and less these days. He was out of control. He needed to stop this madness here and now. Let her go and turn himself in. Almost immediately, his reply to himself was why? Why should he stop? He wouldn't get caught, hell he couldn't get caught. Beside it felt so good, holding the power of life and death in his hands. Knowing that he and only he could save or kill this woman and her baby.

Meanwhile, Sarah lay on the carpet, pushing herself away from the man as best as she could. With no chance of escape, she quickly realised that her best and only chance lay in trying to get help and with this thought in mind, she started to scream at the top of her lungs.

This startled the man out of his thoughts and inner turmoil and into motion. He marched over to her and swung his right foot into her face, bursting her nose and breaking at least one tooth. Sarah's head snapped back against the wall knocking her out. The man then bent down and started to pick his fallen victim up. Once he had her fully in his arms he moved across the room to the bed, dumping her on top of it. Her body bounced slightly on the mattress before coming to a rest on her side, still unconscious.

The sane side of the man was completely gone for now. It was losing the battle for the man's mind day by day. In moments of clarity, the man cursed the trigger event that had caused this in the first place. The violence and death that the man had been exposed to had been too much for him until finally his mind had snapped.

Bringing himself back to the present, the man rested his left hand on the bump of the unborn baby and started to caress it. His knife was in his right hand, idle at the moment. It wouldn't be for long.

CRIME SCENE # 2

FOUR DAYS LATER

15:16

John Carter watched as the two armed police officers escorted James Black into the back of the armoured police van. He was putting a lot more than his career at risk by arranging for James to get out for his help. His boss Carl Pullman was still in the dark over it. He had called in favours from a friend higher up, and that friend was not very happy about this.

James was dressed in civilian clothes but still had both hands cuffed in front of him. They were about to head over towards Princes Street and the third crime scene. So far James was reserving his opinion until he saw all five crime scenes. It had been the latest murder that had prompted John into making this decision. The deaths of both Brian and Sarah Gray were bad enough in their own right but they had also been gutted and Sarah's unborn child had been removed from the womb. The scene had created an impression of a man out of control, which made him someone they had to stop at all costs.

Once they were satisfied that James was locked up securely in the back of the van the two officers and John climbed into the front to head towards scene number 3.

16:02

The man sat at his desk in his office at work; trying against the odds to do some work. It wasn't happening. The urge to kill was eating away at him again, this time after only four days. He had to do something. His sane side was almost non-existent by this time and he was struggling to regain control long enough to keep up the pretence that he was nothing more than an every day Joe Bloggs.

He might have patterned himself on James Black but he didn't have what it took. It was slowly eating away at him whereas James thrived on it. James could control the urge, but then James wasn't losing his mind whereas he was. Much as he didn't want to admit it, he was losing his grip on reality, the need to kill slowly becoming the most important thing in his life.

CRIME SCENE # 3

OFF PRINCES STREET AT EAST END

16:59

James stood facing Princes Street. He was in a side street beside a fast food restaurant at the east end. The Bridges linking Princes Street with the rest of Edinburgh were just in front of him. This is where the third victim had been killed. In the street and yet there were still no witnesses. James found this puzzling but not impossible after all he had done similar things and gotten away with it.

'Well,' John asked him.

'I'm thinking,' James answered. The two armed officers were at either side of James. The killer's eyes flicked back and forth between the two. Both of the officers had their guns in a holster so as not to draw overly amounts of attention to them and as far as James could tell neither officer had the safety snib on the holster off, so the guns weren't that accessible at a moments notice.

James didn't think that they would be able to get their guns out that fast, but still he needed something else as a backup. He glanced back down Princes Street at the oncoming traffic, making it look like a casual glance, like a man enjoying his last small bit of freedom. Perfect, he thought. A double decker bus was heading his way. He waited a few more seconds while it got closer and then without warning he raised his cuffed hands, clasping them together as he did so and spun round towards one of the officers he was with.

His hands clubbed the officer, knocking him to the ground. The other officer was already fumbling with his gun and John was moving towards him at pace. They really were reacting much faster than he had given them credit for, James thought to himself.

Turning, James ran straight out into the traffic, timed just right so that the bus was bearing right down towards him. Still James ran, never faltering once. The feeling of adrenaline that was flowing through him again for the first time in over a year brought of smile to his lips as he fled.

The driver of the bus slammed hard on the brakes. The bus started to swerve and the tires screeched but James continued onwards, throwing himself towards the other side of the street.

He landed awkwardly amougst several curious onlookers and was quickly scrambling back to his feet, his hands still clasped in front of him.

Back on the other side of the street, John and the two police officers had drawn their weapons but found that the now stopped bus was blocking their view of the opposite side of the street.

'Shit,' John cursed. 'GET AFTER HIM, NOW,' he ordered.

Meanwhile the traffic on Princes Street had turned into chaos as a result of the bus having to do an emergency stop.

John and the officers ran across the street and were now having to fight their way through the crowds as more and more people starting moving towards them to see what all of the commotion was about.

'There he is,' one of the officers shouted out pointing at the figure running up the street.

One of the officers tried to raise his gun to take aim at the escaping killer but had to back down, as there were just too many people in the vicinity.

'Shit,' John cried out in anger.

James was halfway up the bridges ducking in as many large crowds as he could. The logic being that they wouldn't be able to see him as easily or take a shot at him in case they hit an innocent person.

John continued to chase but James was lost in the crowds and he could no longer see him. Reluctantly he had to force himself to think about how to handle this. First off, he would have to accept full responsibility for this but more importantly he would have to report it as soon as possible so that they could try and catch him before he could start a new killing spree.

OUTSIDE OF THE PULLMAN RESIDENCE

18:16

The man sat in his car outside of the house. He'd come here straight from work. He was trying so hard to suppress the urge to kill but it wasn't working. He had to do it. It didn't matter who it was that he was killing anymore and he knew that should there be anyone in the house then they would die.

Knowing that there was no point in fighting the inevitable, the man opened the car door and stepped out. He headed up the pathway leading to the front door of the house. He could see lights on inside, on both floors.

Reaching the front door, he tried the handle. It was unlocked. That was careless of them, he thought. He entered the house and had a quick look around. He could hear someone upstairs moving about and singing to themselves. It was a woman's voice.

After a quick glance around, the man moved to the right doorway into the kitchen and had another look around, his eyes resting on a knife block that was situated beside the cooker. He walked over to it and removed the largest knife in the block. It glistened in the bright light from the overheads.

He could hear the sound of someone coming down the stairs. It was the same someone who had been doing the singing.

Turning around, he started to walk back into the entrance hall. The occupant still didn't know that he was in the house yet and had made her way into the living room.

The man turned to face the living room entrance. He saw the woman who had been doing the singing with her back to him, polishing some pine wooden units that were covered with ornaments. Stepping into the room, the man started to approach her, the knife gripped tightly in his hand.

Karen Pullman was quite happy dusting and singing away to herself, when she felt a presence behind her. Spinning around, she saw the man approaching her. She issued a small scream in fright before relaxing again.

'Carl,' she said. 'You nearly gave me a heart attack.'

THORN RESIDENCE

12TH FLOOR OF TOWERBLOCK FLATS

SIGHTHILL

18:33

'What do you mean, James Black has escaped?' Frank hissed into the phone. He had just answered it a few minutes ago to find a very distressed John Carter on the other end. He listened for a few minutes.

'You took him out of prison, with nothing more than yourself and two armed police officers as an escort. Are you out of your mind? Did it not occur to you that it took years to capture that man and that maybe you should have had more men, or better yet maybe you shouldn't have taken him out at all.'

On the other end of the phone John was trying to keep his temper intact. He could understand why Frank was angry but he was never the less unhappy about taking the brunt of his anger, even though it was his fault.

Frank forced himself to calm down slightly. 'What does Carl have to say about this?' he asked.

'I don't know. I haven't been able to get hold of him since it happened.'

'You have reported it though, haven't you?'

'Of course I have,' John replied angrily. 'There are police officers out there now looking for him.'

'Fat lot of good that will do,' Frank muttered. 'It didn't work last year or four years ago. James is too good at keeping hidden when he wants to.'

'We'll find him,' John reassured Frank.

'Question, Detective,' Frank asked. 'Why did you see fit to tell me this?'

'So that you are prepared in case he comes to finish what he started last year.'

‘Oh. I’m sure that he will try to finish me off unless he’s caught again, but for the time being he doesn’t know that I’m alive. His most likely target at the moment would b…’ he trailed off.

‘Would be who?’ John pressed.

‘Would be Carl,’ Frank continued. ‘It was Carl who captured him last year. It is Carl that he will want to start with. You have to get as many units as possible over to Carl’s now.’

‘Why would he do something as predictable as that so soon after escaping? He would be just as well just turning himself in.’

‘The thrill of getting away with it is part of the fun for James. He has escaped capture so many times from situations with a huge police presence. He’ll probably also believe that you won’t think that he would be as bold as to go for such an obvious target and thus won’t be prepared.’

‘I really don’t think that he would be that daring within hours of his escape. Surely he’d lay low for a day or so, at the very least.’

‘You already said that you can’t get hold of Carl,’ Frank snapped. Even now, after they had seen everything that James was capable of, people still didn’t believe him. ‘Send some units round there. If James isn’t there, fine, but if he does turn up, it’ll be your chance to re-capture him. If nothing else, you’ll be at least able to warn Carl.’

Without waiting for a reply, Frank hung up and grabbed his jacket. He had always known that sooner or later he was going to have to come out of hiding and that as long as James Black was still out there he would never be free.

Catherine came into the room. ‘Where are you going?’ she asked, scared to hear the answer but having to ask all the same.

‘Over to Carl’s. It’s important.’

‘You’re not getting back into the force again, are you? You said that was all over with.’

‘I have to go. You must believe me when I say it’s not something that I want to do, but I have to do it never the less. James Black has escaped. He’s out there now and I think that it will be Carl that he will go for.’

With that he turned and ran out of the flat heading for the lifts. He didn’t live too far from where Carl did. In fact he would probably get there before the other police units, especially if the majority of the units where in the city centre looking for their escaped killer.

LOTHIAN AND BORDERS POLICE STATION

SAME TIME

John sat holding the phone receiver in his hand. Frank had hung up but John was still sitting processing everything that he had just been told. Would James really be brave enough to head straight over to Carl’s place so soon after having escaping custody? He found that hard to believe, but what if Frank was right and it was true that he couldn't reach Carl.

PULLMAN RESIDENCE

18:34

James made his way to the front door of Carl Pullman's home. He had found the address in the phone book and there was only one Carl Pullman in the book, so he had known where to come to. It was going to be a quick job, nothing elaborate like what he had set up to kill Frank last year. He didn't have time. If only Carl was half the man that Frank had been. Frank had posed some competition at least whilst Carl had just gotten lucky a year ago. James had simply made a mistake, he'd let his guard down.

James reached out to open the door. He saw the marks that the cuffs had made on his wrist when he had been removing them. That had been slightly painful but not the worst thing that he'd had to put up with in his life. He was still dressed in the clothes that John Carter had given him for the trip, but he would get a change soon.

He entered the house and saw the living room straight ahead. What he didn't expect to see was the sight of Carl bending over the dead body of a woman with a kitchen knife. Carl was literally gutting the woman.

Carl was so engrossed with what he was doing that he didn't hear the door open and didn't know that James was in the house. The last part of him that had been sane had died when he had killed his wife and all that was left was the out of control madman. Before it was lost the sane side had tried reasoning again. It had pointed out that this wasn't Carl. That Carl wasn't well. He had obsessed over James Black last year whilst he was in charge of the investigation and Frank had been in a coma. But whereas Frank had been able to turn off to the violence that James had done, Carl's mind hadn't been able to deal with it and when James was caught, the images and the dreams didn't stop. Carl had gone slowly but surely mad over time.

'Well, well, well,' James said from behind Carl.

Carl looked up to see who the intruder was, recognising James straight away.

'So I'm betting that you're the copy cat killer, then,' James declared, a smile on his lips. 'This is even better than I had hoped for. I get my revenge and remove the competition in one go.'

Carl stood up, the knife in his hand, a snarl spreading across his face. James could see what was about to happen and tensed for it. Carl lunged across the room at him.

18:38

Frank was driving like a wild man to get to Carl's as quickly as possible. He'd tried phoning Carl's mobile but it was turned off and he didn't have Carl's home number. He just hoped that he wasn't too late.

PULLMAN RESIDENCE

18:39

James threw Carl back against the wall, causing him to drop the knife. Carl might be good at killing defenceless and unsuspecting people but he was hopeless against him. Even during their fight in the school a year ago, it had been a chair that Carl had used to get the better of him.

Carl slumped down against the wall. He tried to get to his feet quickly and launch another attack, but James was too quick for him. He moved across the room and grabbed Carl by the head. One hand at each side of Carl's face, he pulled him back up to his feet, holding him so that his back was still against the wall.

'Did you really think that you were a match for me?' he snarled at his opponent. He moved his grip on Carl's head slightly so that his thumbs were positioned over both of Carl's eyes.

'Time to die,' he muttered. With that he pushed both thumbs forwards into Carl's eyeballs. With his back up against the wall, there was no way that Carl could try to move away from this.

James felt some resistance from the eyes but that soon gave way as he increased the pressure that he was exhorting on them. Carl screamed out in pain unable to stop what was happening. Seconds later James's thumbs were covered in the slime and bloody pulp that was released from Carl's eyeballs. Carl tried kicking out at him but it had no effect. James continued to push forwards.

18:40

Frank's car skidded to a standstill outside of Carl's house. He had been right. He had gotten here before the police. That was assuming that John Carter had ordered the units over here. He got out of the car and started to run up the path to the front door. He was about to ring the doorbell when he realised that the door was already swinging ajar.

Frank realised that he wasn't even armed and that he was about to enter a house that potentially had a serial killer inside of it.

Pushing the door fully open, he stepped inside. The door started to swing closed so that it would lie ajar once again.

The living room door in front of him was closed too, but he could hear a commotion coming from behind it. Suddenly he heard Carl scream out in pain.

Without waiting any more, Frank burst into the living room, pushing the door wide open as he did so.

'CARL,' he cried out. What he saw was like a butcher's shop. Carl's wife dead on the floor, Carl himself pinned up against the wall by James who had both of his thumbs in Carl's eye sockets. Carl was thrashing about and screaming out in pain every so often.

James heard and recognised the voice although he couldn't place it straight away. He turned round to face the new comer. The look of surprise on his face when he saw who it was, quickly changed into one of anger and hatred.

'You,' he hissed. 'Alive and well, I see.'

His interest in Carl disappeared entirely at this point. With a quick move of his hands he snapped Carl's neck and threw the body down the carpet like a child throwing a rag doll away.

Frank was frozen to the spot, suddenly aware that he had no idea what the hell he was going to do.

James moved around to face Frank square on. With one at each end of the room they faced each other.

PART 4

EDINBURGH

1985

14:01

The fourteen-year-old James Black fell back against the wall of the empty school dining room. He had been punched in the face by another kid called Martin Dilved. Martin had been bullying James for the better part of three months now. In fact, since Martin had transferred to this school he had quickly made friends with some of the school's worst troublemakers and had decided in his wisdom that he was going to target select people to try and make himself look big and important. James was one of these select people. Two of Martin's friends were standing at the side cheering him on.

James tried to straighten up again but received another punch, this time in the stomach. He doubled over in pain, the wind knocked out of him. His legs buckled and he collapsed to the ground.

'Look at him crawling,' one of Martin's friends named Jake said.

James reached out towards Martin's feet and was able to grab his ankle and pull Martin down to the ground too. Before he could do anything else however, Jake had reached down, grabbing James to give Martin time to get back up to his feet.

James continued to struggle against Jake and was finally able to free himself but by this time Martin was upright again.

'You think you're a smart ass?' Martin hissed at him, trying to regain his composure after being brought down to the ground by his chosen victim. That wasn't ever meant to happen and if left unchecked could dent his reputation. He swung his foot out at James, kicking him in the groin.

James immediately felt bolts of pain lance upwards through his body and he buckled over again, dropping down to the floor like a brick, his hands moving over towards his privates. He could feel the sting of tears in his eyes and he readied himself for the next blow that he knew would be on its way.

'Someone's coming,' Martin's other friend, Rick, called out. 'Come on. We have to go.'

Martin turned round to the fallen James. 'You're lucky,' he said. 'We'll finish this off later.'

With that Martin and his two friends turned and left the dining room through one of the side doors, leaving James to pull himself back to his feet. The main door to the dining room opened and an elderly cleaning woman entered pushing a cleaning trolley in front of her. Upon seeing James she paused.

'Should you not be in class?' she asked.

James glared in response to this but didn't say anything. The cleaning lady took a closer look at him, seeing a trickle of blood running down from the corner of his mouth.

'You all right son?' she asked.

'I'm fine,' James said as he grabbed his school bag off the floor and stormed past her. His pride was as hurt as he was physically. This would not happen again, he promised himself. He wouldn't let it and as for Martin and his two friends. They would regret the day that they screwed with him. The whole school would learn the hard way. He'd make sure of it.

CRAWFORD RESIDENCE

16:17

James entered the house as quietly as he possibly could. He wanted to be able to sneak past his abusive stepfather, Mark. James and Mark had never gotten on. Every time that James had stepped out of line, he had had hell to pay, usually in the form of a beating.

James had learned that he had been adopted four years ago, when his mother had felt that he was old enough to know the truth. He had been adopted at the age of one by Jeff and Sandra Black. Jeff Black died when James had been only been five years old. Two years later Sandra had met and married Mark Crawford.

From that moment onwards James's home life had been hell, as Mark wasn't stupid enough to do anything in front of Sandra. As a result Sandra felt that James was just trying to get attention by claiming that Mark hit him.

Nine months ago the situation had gotten worse, when Sandra died from a heart attack. Now there was no one to protect James and Mark was his legal guardian. Mark blamed everything that went wrong on James and administered beatings to make his point. Mark even blamed Sandra's death on James, even though he knew that it was just one of those things.

LATE 2002

PULLMAN RESIDENCE

18:40

The living room door in front of him was closed too, but he could hear a commotion coming from behind it. Suddenly he heard Carl scream out in pain.

Without waiting any more, Frank burst into the living room, pushing the door wide open as he did so.

'CARL,' he cried out. What he saw was like a butcher's shop. Carl's wife dead on the floor, Carl himself pinned up against the wall by James who had both of his thumbs in Carl's eye sockets. Carl was thrashing about and screaming out in pain every so often.

James heard and recognised the voice although he couldn't place it straight away. He turned round to face the new comer. The look of surprise on his face when he saw who it was, quickly changed into one of anger and hatred.

'You,' he hissed. 'Alive and well, I see.'

His interest in Carl disappeared entirely at this point. With a quick move of his hands he snapped Carl's neck and threw the body down the carpet like a child throwing a rag doll away.

Frank was frozen to the spot, suddenly aware that he had no idea what the hell he was going to do.

James moved around to face Frank square on. With one at each end of the room they faced each other.

'You didn't have to kill his wife,' Frank said stalling for time hoping that the police cars would get here very soon.

James smiled at this. 'I would love to take the credit for his wife but I'm afraid that I can't. Carl did that himself. He's your copy cat killer.'

'What,' Frank asked, not believing it.

'Now its time to finish off business between us,' James hissed as he started to move forward.

1985

James was in the school boiler room, splashing petrol about the place. He'd thrown anything even remotely flammable around the place. He'd covered the boiler with petrol and started to make a trail of it out of the room and into the hallway outside. The classes were in at the moment and the corridors were empty. Lighting a match, James threw it at the beginning of the petrol trail.

Instantly flames leapt up and started to eat away at the spilt fuel. The fire started moving faster, tearing into the boiler room.

James turned and started to walk away from the blaze, heading towards the entrance at a casual but never the less effective pace.

Inside the rest of the building both teachers and pupils were blissfully unaware of what was about to happen to them. The teachers taught and lectured their pupils. Some took heed of their lesions whilst others like Martin and his friends ignored them.

Down in the boiler room, the fire was raging and had engulfed the boiler and everything else in the room.

Meanwhile, James was walking down the school driveway. He continued walking once he got out of the premises and started to head home.

Inside of the building, the boiler finally blew. The explosion tore through the ceiling above it and a huge fireball erupted upwards, engulfing everything that it passed. The building shook under the explosion and seconds later the fire alarms started ringing.

Electrical fires were also starting to break out now through the building as well. The teachers tried to evacuate their pupils and some were able to do so easily, whereas the classrooms above and around the boiler room were blazing infernos with all inside being roasted alive by the flames.

Some minutes later, the first of the fire engines turned up.

CRAWFORD RESIDENCE

THREE HOURS LATER

Mark watched as the two police officers left in their police car. They had come to check on James after he hadn't been present at the roll call of pupils. They had feared that he was one of the children that the fire brigade hadn't been able to get out. When they realised that he was ok they wanted to know why he wasn't there.

James had told them that he was skipping classes, which he did on a fairly regular basis and that if they wanted to check that up with the teachers then that was fine, because they were always giving him detentions for skipping his classes and again for not attending his detentions.

Mark turned round to face James. 'Kind of lucky that you weren't in that building; wasn't it?'

'Yeah. It was,' James replied.

'You're not holding something back are you?' Mark asked.

'No,' James replied. 'Why? What are you implying?'

Mark moved across the hallway fast, lashing out at James when he reached him. James was knocked to the floor.

'I'll ask the questions boy,' he said. 'I better not find out that you had anything to do with that fire or I'll turn you in myself. You understand me?'

James glared up at his stepfather, but nodded his understanding.

'Good,' Mark replied. 'Now go to your room. I don't want to see you again for the rest of the night.'

James got back up to his feet and marched up the stairs. He couldn't wait for the day when either his stepfather died or when he'd be old enough to actually strike back, but at the moment he would have to bide his time.

LATE 2002
PULLMAN RESIDENCE

18:41

James moved across the room fast. Frank tried to back off but his back hit the doorframe and James grabbed him. Spinning him around, James threw Frank into the centre of the room. Frank stumbled in an effort to keep his balance, but lost all chance of that when he hit the body of Carl's dead wife, Karen. He fell down on top of the body.

'Imagine keeping yourself hidden all this time. I am impressed, but now we can start to have fun again, just like the good old days,' James said to his fallen opponent.

On the carpet, Frank caught sight of the kitchen knife that Carl had used to kill his wife. He had to get hold of it.

1998

PARKEN RESIDENCE

10:00

Detective Frank Thorn stood standing in the crime scene. There was a chalk outline where the body had been and the techs had already been through the place with a fine toothcomb but Frank knew fine well that they wouldn't find anything that would help them find the killer.

The victim this time had been a young black woman. She had literally had her gullet ripped out of her throat.

Frank turned and started to walk away. He had lost count as to how many victims this made. There seemed to be no connection to the victims and the only pattern that the killer used was the level of violence that he displayed when he killed.

His boss, Robert Platt was demanding that this killer be caught but although they had fingerprints, hair and fibre it wasn't helping. The killer didn't have a previous record and they were no closer to catching him. If they did catch him, they could prove that he committed the crimes without a shadow of doubt but until they caught him, they were screwed.

TWO AND A HALF WEEKS LATER

KINGHORNE AND ZAHN RESIDENCE

21:03

Joyce Kinghorne and Pat Zahn entered the house that they shared with one and other. They had just come back from shopping as they had used the last of their food the night before.

They were both students in their early twenties. The house actually belonged to Joyce's father but he was working abroad at the moment and was allowing Joyce to stay in it. Joyce in turn had asked Pat, one of her long-term friends to share it with her in an effort to half the bills.

It was an arrangement that suited them both as Pat's parents lived in Glasgow and she didn't really want to live in the halls of residence.

They entered the hallway and closed the front door behind them. Joyce had all of the groceries with her split into two bags.

'Don't just stand there,' Joyce said to Pat. 'Get the lights, so that I can see what I'm doing.'

'Oh. Sorry,' Pat mumbled before reaching for the light switch and flicking it to the on position. Nothing happened. She tried the switch next to it for the upstairs light. Once again, nothing happened.

'I'm waiting,' Joyce said to her friend.

'Nothing's happening,' Pat replied. 'The fuse must have tripped or something.'

'Terrific,' Joyce muttered. 'Okay. I'll dump the food and go and look at the fuse board, since we both know how electrically minded you are.'

'Screw you,' Pat came back at her, laughing as she did so.

Joyce started to slowly walk through to the kitchen, dumping the bags of groceries on the floor once she got there. She started to feel her way towards the kitchen utility cupboard where she kept her torch.

Meanwhile Pat moved slowly into the living room, where light from the moon illuminated the room to a slight extent. She flopped into one of the chairs to wait for the lights to come back on.

James watched her from behind the living room door. He'd heard them both come back in from their shopping trip and he was readying himself for the kill. His knife was still in its sheath on his belt, but that wasn't important at the moment. In his right hand he was holding a large hook. The point sharpened to a tee.

Feeling the adrenaline flowing through him in anticipation of the kill, he stepped out from behind the door, pushing it closed as he did so. He moved fast across the room to reach his intended victim before she could scream out.

Pat sensed rather than saw the movement but it was too late. As she started to turn towards it, James had grabbed her by the throat, with his left hand, to cut off her call for help. Holding her steady on her feet, he raised the large hook over his head in a menacing stance. The look of fear in her face was all that he needed to encourage him. He brought the hook down into Pat's face.

The point pierced through Pat's eye and started to move easily through the lower brain, meeting some resistance at her upper mouth. Pat was killed instantly. With the body stuck like a fish on a hook, James hauled it towards him and sidestepped it at the last moment releasing his grip on the hook as he did so. The momentum carried the body into the wall where it crashed with a thump. The body slid down to the carpet. Without taking his eyes of the sight of the sliding body James pulled his knife out of its sheath.

In the kitchen, Joyce had the torch in her hands and was looking at the trip switches. She heard the thump from the next room.

'Pat,' she called out. 'What are you doing?'

When she didn't get any reply, she turned back to the fuses. The red master switch had indeed tripped. She flicked it back to the ON position and immediately the hallway was flooded in light.

Getting back up, she laid the torch on the table. 'Pat,' she called out.

'What was the thump?' She left the kitchen to head towards the living room and her friend to get an explanation.

Inside of the living room, James had ripped open Pat's stomach cavity and was using the blood from the wound to write his name on the wall. This was his message to the police, his taunt to them. He would see how far this would get them.

Meanwhile Joyce had now reached the living room, pushed open the door and flicked the light on as she entered. 'Pat,' she said again. 'Are you deaf or somet…' She trailed off when she saw the bloody mess on the carpet.

James spun round to face her. He knew that she was coming but had been busy finishing his scrawl on the living room wall. He raised the knife and swung out at her, but she was out of reach and faster to react to the carnage than he would have given her credit for.

Screaming out, she jumped backwards the way that she had come. Without wasting any time she turned from the killer and headed towards the front door.

'Please don't be locked,' she muttered to no one in particular. The handle turned and the door opened. Pat quickly moved through the opening and entered the front garden. She had to get help fast. James was leaving the living room and wasn't far behind her as she left the house.

She ran into a neighbour's garden across the road and up their pathway, all the while screaming out for help. Upon reaching the neighbour's front door, she started to hammer on it with her fists.

James was by now on the far side of the road and stepping off the pavement towards her.

WESTERN RESIDENCE

21:12

Fred and Christina Western were babysitting their grandson Jason, for their daughter. The baby was only three months old and already the pride and joy of the whole family. Their daughter was being taken out by her husband for the first time since the boy was born and they probably wouldn't be back until at least eleven p.m. but Fred and Christina didn't mind. They relished the opportunity to spend time with their grandson.

Currently they were sitting in the living room watching the television while the baby boy was sleeping in his pram. They kept checking on him to make sure that he was alright and that he didn't need anything but so far he had slept soundly. The perfect little angel. The perfect addition to their whole family. They really couldn't be happier. It never crossed their minds how quickly things could change. How in a matter of seconds their whole lives could be turned upside down.

The two of them jumped when the thumps started at their front door. The sound of screaming was filtering through too. They looked at each other across the room, looks of concern passing between them.

'What the hell,' Fred muttered, getting up and leaving to see who was at the door. Jason woke to the noise and started to cry. Christina went over to him and picked him up from his pram to try and sooth him into going back to sleep.

Outside, James had now reached the same side of the road that Joyce was on and was only a few feet away from entering the front garden. Joyce glanced behind her to see James rapidly closing the distance.

'OPEN UP, PLEASE,' she cried out at the neighbour's door. 'HELP ME.'

Fred reached his front door and opened it to see what all the fuss was about. Joyce practically fell into his hallway, slamming the door closed behind her and turning the keys in the locks as she did so.

'What the hell do you think you're doing?' Fred demanded, having not seen James in his garden.

'Call the police,' she replied. 'He killed her. Call the police now.'

By this time Christina was in the hallway as well, the quieting form of Jason in her arms.

'What are you talking about?' Fred asked. 'Whose been killed?'

Before Joyce could answer, there came a heavy thump from the door. Joyce yelped in fright and fear. 'CALL THE POLICE,' she screamed.

'Christina. Go and phone the police,' Fred ordered, not knowing what was happening but knowing enough to know that he was out of his depth.

'What's going on?' she asked.

'Just do it,' he came back at her.

Meanwhile the thumps and crashes from the other side of the door continued and intensified. The wood on the inside was beginning to split and the point of James Black's knife could be seen as he raised it and brought it into the door time and time again. The door wouldn't hold much longer at this rate.

Christina was now through in the kitchen to get the phone that hung on the wall there.

Outside, James had stopped attacking the door with his knife and re-sheathed it for now. Turning his attention back to the weakened panel of the door that he'd been hitting, he pulled his fist back and took a swing at it.

The wood cracked further under the force of his fist, but held never the less. He took another swing. This time the panel buckled and his fist burst through. He began to push his hand further in, scrambling for the locks on the inside as he did so.

Realising what this intruder was trying to do Fred dashed forward to remove the key from the lock, but it was too late. James found the key just before Fred could get there and turned it round. The deadbolts inside of the door gave a heavy thud as he did so. With his other hand on the outside of the door, James turned the handle and pushed the door open, pulling his hand back out of the hole, so that he would be fully mobile when he entered.

Fred tried to block his way. 'Who the hell do you thin…' he started before he was cut off by James's left hand grabbing him by the throat and pushing up against the wall.

Joyce stood paralysed in the hallway, her strength and resolve gone. Part of her wanted to help this man who'd she'd never even spoken to before tonight, the other part of her wanted to run as fast as she could.

In the kitchen, Christina finished her call to the police, laid baby Jason - who was screaming out again- down on the unit and went back into the hallway to see what the hell was going on.

Pulling his knife back out of its sheath, James raised it above the terrified face of Fred and brought it down hard. The blade burst through Fred's eye and entered his brain, killing him.

'FRED,' Christina called out in despair.

Joyce finally started to move back into action. She grabbed Christina by the arm. 'Come on. We have to leave now. Where's your back door?'

Christina was still in shock at the sight of her husband being killed like this right in front of her and even Joyce grabbing her by the arm didn't help her move. It wasn't until James pulled the knife back out from Fred's eye socket and turned round to face them that she realised that she still had her grandson to think about.

Christina moved back into the kitchen, pulling Joyce with her. James started to follow, the blood from the knife blade dripping onto the hall carpet as he went. Once in the kitchen, Christina ran towards her grandson.

Aware that time was running out, James lashed out without warning, swinging out with the knife. Joyce jumped back to try and avoid it but her back hit a kitchen bunker that she hadn't seen as she was backing away instead of running away.

The blade missed her but James was able to reach her because of the bunker slowing her down. Having reached her grandson, Christina was picking him up in her arms. She turned back round in time to see Joyce getting her throat slashed open and the gush of blood pouring out onto the kitchen floor as her body collapsed.

With Joyce now dead, James now turned to face Christina and started to menacingly walk towards her. The crying of the baby was starting to get on his nerves. Christina backed away into the corner, holding baby Jason tight to her chest.

'Please. No,' Christina pleaded with him.

James reached out for the baby but Christina shied away from him to try and protect Jason.

'You're only postponing the inevitable,' James told her. 'You're both going to die tonight.'

With that he lashed out at Christina with his fist. It hit her in the face and knocked back hard against the corner unit that she had backed away into. She collapsed to the floor, stunned by the blow and her nose starting to bleed. James reached down for Jason and before Christina knew what was happening he had plucked the baby out of her arms and was standing holding him up at head level.

'So small,' he muttered to himself. He glanced around the room, his eyes coming to rest on a microwave sitting in the corner. A smile started to spread out across his face and he re-sheathed his knife.

Walking over to the unit that the microwave was on top of, he opened the door. It would be a tight fit but he was pretty sure that he could get the baby inside of it.

Christina had recovered enough from the punch to realise what was about to happen to her grandson. She got back up to her feet and rushed at the killer. Reaching him, she threw herself at his back.

James turned back to face her. Jason held tightly in his left hand by the collar of his nightclothes, hanging in mid-air. With his right hand, James once again lashed out at Christina, again hitting her in the face and again knocking her back down to the floor. To ensure no further interruptions from her, he kicked her in the stomach as hard as he could forcing the wind out of her. Throughout all this, Jason was crying out loud and it was grating on James's nerves. He swung another kick at Christina.

She tried to cry out in pain but all she could manage was a gasp, still struggling to get air. James turned his attention back to the microwave and started to place baby Jason inside of it, manoeuvring his small arms and legs to make him fit.

The killer then closed the door and started to look over the controls. Finding the power setting, he turned it up to MAX and then turned the timer to 30 MINS. All that was needed was for him to press the START button.

Christina had managed to crawl over to where James was standing. She reached out and grasped his ankle, trying to pull him away or at least distract him long enough for the police to arrive. Looking down at her, James pulled his ankle free and reached out for the button.

'NO,' Christina cried out and she made one final effort to stop him. Grabbing his ankle again to try and give herself a bit of leverage, she sunk her teeth into the side of his calf.

This got the killer's full attention and he pulled back from the microwave, trying to wrench his leg free from her.

'Bitch,' he called out. He swung his other foot into her face, forcing her to release her grip on him.

Turning to the fallen woman, he bent down and hauled her to her feet, throwing her against the far unit once he had done so. He pulled his knife back out of its sheath and started to close the gap between himself and Christina.

James abruptly paused in his tracks. In the distance, the sound of police sirens could be heard. He was caught between two minds. Did he have enough time to finish this off without being caught? It was a chance that he wasn't willing to take at least not when he had gone to the bother of setting up his taunt.

Turning to the badly beaten Christina, he smiled at her. 'You're lucky I'm pressed for time,' he said to her.

With that, he turned and ran back down the hallway past the dead body of Fred and back out of the front door. Within seconds he was gardens away, keeping to the shadows.

Back in the kitchen, Christina pulled herself to her feet and stumbled over to the microwave. She opened the appliance door to get her grandson back out. Tears were running down her face at the memory of her husband dying, at how close she had come to losing her grandson and at how close she had come to dying herself. Her hands were literally shaking. The first of the police cars pulled up outside seconds later.

POLICE STATION

01:33

Frank watched as Christina Western was reunited with her daughter. The two embraced and the tears started straight away. One crying for a husband and the other for her father. Baby Jason was being checked out in the local hospital as a precaution and would soon be released back to the parents if nothing was wrong.

He turned away to leave them to their grief in privacy. Christina had worked with a police sketch artist and had given their first real clue as to how they might catch the killer.

All searches against the name, James Black had revealed nothing useful. They couldn't find any records of anyone living in the Edinburgh area with that name, no driving license, no voting registration, no passport records and so forth.

His best bet, he felt was the artist impression. He went back into his office to arrange for the picture to be shown on the news and in newspapers. He also wanted to have wanted posters made up for display in every police station. Finally he had to get a help line set up for the public to phone in should they have any information about the man in the picture.

FOUR DAYS LATER

11:39

Frank was heading round to a branch of one of Edinburgh's largest banks. They had had a call on the hotline from a Sally Nicholson. She had reported that she had seen and served the man in the picture earlier that day and now Frank wanted to speak to her personally and check out the CCTV tapes from the bank too.

POLICE STATION

14:20

Frank had just gotten back from the bank. Their security tapes confirmed that James had indeed been in the bank. They had hoped for more information from a bank account but it turns out he was only getting change. When the bank manager was asked to look up any accounts under the name James Black, none came up. The manager had agreed to allow Frank to place an undercover officer in the bank should James return. The officer was under specific instructions not to approach the killer if he returns but to call for back up straight away.

TWO DAYS LATER

12:59

James walked into the bank, his eyes moving round across the lines of cashiers until he found the one that he wanted. Sally Nicholson. He had a ten-pound note in his hands that he was going to ask for change with. He moved into her queue, bypassing some of the shorter lines for service.

He wondered if the police had cottoned on to this yet. He was going to show them exactly who they were messing with. He had deliberately entered the bank once he had seen his face on T.V. and he was pretty sure that Sally would have contacted them once she had seen the news. He was going to let them know in advance of whom he was going to go for next and then he was going to kill her despite their best efforts to stop him. This would prove his point that he was much smarter than they were.

The undercover officer sat beside the cashiers with an 'IN TRAINING' sign at his side and someone behind him showing him what to do. He glanced up and saw James in the queue.

'Shit,' he muttered to himself. He turned to the person behind him and asked to be let off to the toilet. Once he was in the back where the customers couldn't see him, he grabbed hold of the nearest telephone and dialled the number that he'd been given to report that the man they wanted was here. A few minutes later he was finished and he moved back to take his post at the IN TRAINING sign, so as not to draw attention to himself. When he got back he looked around for James but couldn't see him anywhere. Where had he gone? He looked around from queue to queue but couldn't see him anywhere. He had left the building.

A couple of streets away, James was walking away. He'd seen the trainee cashier make eye contact with him and then excuse himself and move through to the back. The police he now knew for sure were on to him. That was good. Even if that trainee wasn't a cop, he would probably phone the police to report that the man on T.V. had entered the bank and was there still.

With his plan starting to come together, he decided to move on to the next stage.

15:13

Frank was cursing their bad luck. They had almost had him. They could have ended it then and there. The police had arrived shortly after the call from the bank as they had been standing by should the call be made.

However by the time they had gotten here, the suspect was gone. He had spent the last few hours reviewing the security tapes and interviewing Sally

Nicholson. He felt that it was safe to assume that James had an interest in her. He felt that it was also safe to assume that James would be keeping track of her outside of the bank as well. It was only a matter of time until he went for her.

When Sally had first phoned in days earlier, he thought that James might have an account with the bank but once that had been disproved he'd wondered why James would expose himself to the public light like that.

From that he had thought that maybe James was tracking his next victim. That was why he had arranged for the undercover officer to be present. He had not however, told Sally of his suspicions. This latest move by the killer re-enforced this suspicion and now he had finally come clean to tell Sally that he thought that she was in danger and would she be willing to use that to help them capture this serial killer before he could kill again?

After some persuasion, Sally had agreed to become the unwilling bait. Even then, the only reason that she did this was because it was explained to her that if she was his next target, then her life was in danger, regardless.

Frank now had to explain all of this to his boss, Robert Platt. He shouldn't be too unhappy about it. They were, after all making progress on the case for the first time since it started.

SIX DAYS LATER

THE ENTRANCE TO 'SPRINGFIELD VIEW'

SOUTH QUEENSFERRY

(OUTSKIRTS OF EDINBURGH)

17:00

James stood in the thick bushes at the entrance to the street that Sally lived in. He could see her house in the distance and he could also see several plain cars that had been there all day, with people in them. Good, he thought. The police are playing right into the game. At the distance he was at, he couldn't make out how many police officers there were outside, plus it was starting to get dark but that didn't matter. He had been watching her house all day and he knew that there were two policemen in the house as well. Sally had come home from work early today and had been inside of her home for the last few hours. James glanced down at his feet. He had a woman tied up and gagged there. She had been there with him since he had gotten there at just after nine in the morning.

Her name was Carol Platt. He had tracked her down and kidnapped her that morning after her husband Robert went to work. It hadn't been hard to track him down and it wasn't hard to find out where he lived. He'd gotten Robert's name as well as Frank's name from the news reports, both on T.V.

and in the papers. It was now time to show them who was running things here.

'Show time,' he said to the woman on the ground. He pulled out a mobile phone that he had found in her handbag when he had taken her. He turned it on and navigated into the handset's phone book. Scrolling down, he eventually found the name of the person he was wanting, ROBERT WORK.

Smiling, James pressed the 'call' button and waited for the phone to be answered.

LOTHIAN AND BORDERS POLICE STATION

17:06

Robert Platt hung the phone up, his face ashen from the news that he had just heard. A whirlwind of thoughts were going through his head. The bastard, James Black was in his house holding his wife captive. He hadn't believed him until he had been able to speak to his wife. She had begged for help and had confirmed that they were in the house.

Cursing the killer and to a certain extent, Frank for not foreseeing this, he picked his phone back up and dialled through to Frank's mobile number.

When he had finished his call, he left his desk and ran out of the office to the car park. He had to help his wife.

NICHOLSON RESIDENCE

17:07

Frank pressed the 'end' button on his mobile and reached for the police radio that was sitting on the table in front of him. He pressed the transmit button and started to speak into it.

'Suspect is at the house of Robert Platt. All units head out to the following address now,' he ordered as he gave the address to the officers.

Sally listened to this and immediately approached Frank. 'What about me?' she asked.

Frank paused. There was something else happening here but he had his orders to send the police officers round to Robert's place. He had arranged for some of these more specialist officers to be armed for this operation due to the uniqueness of the situation. He came to a decision.

'I'm going to leave you two of the armed police officers to keep watch. One at each outer door, there is no point trying to pretend that we aren't here anymore because I think that he already knows.'

'What does that mean?' Sally asked.

Frank shook his head, regretting making the statement. 'I don't know,' he replied. 'Maybe nothing.'

ENTRANCE TO 'SPRINGFIELD VIEW'

17:09

James watched from the bushes as the plain police cars hurtled past him and away from Sally's house. He smiled and nodded his approval at the situation.

He turned round to look back down at Carol, who he had gagged again.

'You did well,' he said to her. 'But I'm afraid that I'm still going to have to kill you. Your husband and this Detective Thorn must know whom they are dealing with.'

With that he pulled his knife out of its sheath, pressed it up against her throat and slashed it open. The blood began to pour out straight away, pooling into the already damp soil. The puddle began to expand and started to move outwards.

James re-sheathed the knife and left the bushes, climbing over a small brick wall that ran down the side of the bushes. He could see a police officer standing at the front door of Sally's house. There would probably be one round the back as well. No problem, he thought to himself. He would take one out and then the other.

PLATT RESIDENCE

17:31

Frank's car pulled up along with the rest of the police cars, in time to see Robert Platt come back out of his house, a piece of paper clutched in his hand. His face was pale with worry. Getting out of the car, Frank ran up to his superior.

'What happened?' he asked. The only answer he got was the shake of Robert's head. A few seconds later Robert held out the piece of paper for Frank to read. Frank took it off him and looked down at it. Four simple words were scrawled over the paper but their meaning was immediately clear.

BETTER LUCK NEXT TIME.

'Shit,' Frank muttered. 'Back in the cars,' he ordered. 'He's at Sally Nicholson's.'

The police officers all dashed back into their cars and started to move back the way that they had come.

Robert moved towards the passenger side of Frank's car. 'I'm coming with you. We're going to get that son of a bitch together and we're going to get my wife back alive. Is that understood?'

Frank nodded his understanding, but was starting to feel that maybe Robert was too personally involved to make a sound judgement of what needed to be done.

NICHOLSON RESIDENCE

17:46

James threw Sally down to the living room floor. He had only gotten into the house just short of ten minutes ago. He had had to dispose of the police officers at both doors without alerting either Sally, the neighbours or in the instance of the first officer, the one at the other door. This had taken more time than he had thought it would, but the result was the same.

James had then picked the lock of the back door, entered the house and after finding Sally in the living room, he had spent the last few minutes beating her up but now the time for fun and games was at an end, he had to finish the job as the police officers were no doubt on their way back having realised that they had been tricked.

He pulled his knife out of its sheath and was readying for the final fatal blow. Suddenly the whole living room lit up with the headlights of the first of the returning police cars. The beams from the headlights were lancing through the large living room window. Seconds later more joined them. James backed away from the light, temporarily blinded by it. There came a thump from the front door, which had been locked by Sally after Frank and the other officers had left earlier on.

This was followed by another thump as the police officers threw themselves at the door to break it in. They had obviously found the dead body of their colleague in the rose bed to the right of the front door.

James looked down at his intended victim and again, raised his knife to deal the fatal blow when he heard the cracking sound as the front door gave way and the sound of the first police officers entering could be heard.

'Fuck,' he muttered, lowering and grudgingly re-sheathing his knife. He took a step backwards to the back of the room. The living room door burst open and the first three officers entered.

'There he is,' one of them shouted.

Before they could do anything however, James took a run forward at the living room window, launching himself off of the ground at the last moment. He hit the window with his shoulder and the glass shattered outwards onto the drive outside. James hit the ground on his side and using his momentum to roll over back to his feet, he scrambled upright again. As he did, he could see more police officers moving towards him, Frank Thorn and Robert Platt amongst them.

Wasting no time, James took off across the street and down a small side path that ran between two gardens. Jumping over a small fence, he found himself in someone's garden. He continued to dart from garden to garden angling back towards the entrance to the street and his chance of freedom.

Behind him, several police officers gave chase. The man leading the chase was Robert Platt, driven by his determination to find out what had happened to his wife.

Frank saw the direction that the killer was heading in and raced back to his car, calling back the officers to him. They broke off the chase and returned to their vehicles. They could get to the entrance to the street faster in a car and they would hopefully be able to cut him off there.

The only man who didn't break off the chase was Robert. He continued chasing James and was slowly closing the gap as his adrenaline level was giving him the energy needed to keep up.

James reached the entrance to the street and swung left on to the Bo-Ness road, which was the main road in the area. The first of the police cars spun out from Springfield View not far behind him. The police cars giving chase forced Robert to throw himself to the side to avoid being hit. He hit his shoulder off of a small brick wall beside some bushes.

Meanwhile, James veered off of the pavement onto a small pedestrian footpath, that the cars couldn't follow him on. The cars came to a screeching halt and the officers jumped out to follow him, Frank amongst them. Within seconds there were more than ten police officers giving pursuit. Only one of them left that was armed, a specialist police sniper named David Walker. He had originally been placed across the street from Sally's house with a view of the front door so that if needed he could take the kill shot from the distance using his rifle but he had lost his placement when he had been ordered to Robert Platt's house with the rest of the officers. Now, he too, gave chase with his sniper rifle in his hands, which was something that he should not do but he was caught up in the moment and with his determination to catch this monster.

James darted to his left and stared to climb a steep grassy embankment, which led to the beginnings of the pedestrian access across the Forth Road Bridge at the top. The officers were still giving chase but some of them slid on the wet grass and toppled back down to the footpath below. James however kept his footing and continued to get closer to his final escape step by step.

Back at the entrance of Springfield View, Robert was pulling himself back up to his feet. He was wheezing from the exertion of the chase. In the distance he could see the police officers moving up the embankment following the killer as he tried to make his escape. He was about to run over and assist them when he saw something out of the corner of his eye. He turned to have a closer look. It was a hand sticking out from the bushes. An icy fear hit him. Please don't be her? He thought to himself. Unable to stop himself, he reached out and parted the branches to reveal the dead body of his wife.

FORTH ROAD BRIDGE

The Forth road bridge spanned across the murky sea called the "Firth Of Forth". It started at the very edge of South Queensferry and made landfall several miles later in North Queensferry and the beginnings of Fife.

Now on the bridge itself, James was heading towards Fife and safety. Running along the pedestrian path at the side of the bridge, he lost his footing slightly and had to grasp the steel railing which ran down the side of the walkway to steady himself again. His muscles were starting to ache slightly but not enough to slow him down yet.

The winds whipped about the running killer as he fled towards the other side of the bridge and freedom. Above him, dark clouds threatened rain at any moment.

To the right of the road bridge stood the Forth Rail Bridge, built over a hundred years previously and still standing proud and tall. Floodlights illuminated the rail bridge giving it a dark yellow glow in the dark winter evening.

Behind him Frank and the other officers were just getting to the top of the embankment and seeing where he was heading they followed him onto the bridge, a new burst of determined energy to reach the madman before he could escape drove Frank and the others to start running faster than they thought they could.

Knowing that it was becoming unlikely that he was going to be able to lose his pursuers, James had to start coming up with a backup and it only took him a second to do so. In front of him, he could see a woman with a young boy, holding him by the hand. They had been walking down the pedestrian walkway towards him, but seeing all the commotion, they had stopped in their tracks. James pulled his knife back out of his sheath.

The mother and her son were unsure what the hell to do. They could see someone running along the pathway towards them and a group of people chasing him and shouting out.

Tightening his grip on the knife handle James put out a final burst of speed towards the woman and her child. She finally saw the knife in his hand and starting to scream, she turned and started to pull her son after her away from the killer.

Before she could get more than a metre away her son tripped over his feet and fell to the ground, having not been ready for what he had been required to do. The woman turned round to her son.

'Come on. Get up,' she shrieked but it was too late. Even as the kid got upright again, James had reached them. Before she could even react, he had punched her in the face, knocking her down to the ground and had grabbed the boy. He picked him up, held the knife against the boy's throat and turned round to face the police. The boy started crying and screaming for help.

'THAT'S FAR ENOUGH,' James shouted at the approaching officers.

They all stopped where they were. Frank came out to the front of the group.

'LET THE BOY GO,' he ordered the killer, who just grinned and continued backing away across the bridge.

'ANY CLOSER AND THE BOY DIES,' James shouted back. Frank paused where he was. He hadn't come this close to let the killer get away. He had to do something.

Back on the embankment, Robert Platt climbed to the top and started heading towards the group of police officers on the bridge. His determination to kill the bastard who'd taken his Carol from him was what was driving him now.

He found the man that he was looking for, David Walker. Marching up to him he shoved other officers out of the way.

'Take him down,' Robert ordered David.

'Sir?' David questioned. 'He has a hostage sir.'

'You have your orders. Just do it.'

'Sir…,' David started to protest again.

'Now,' Robert hissed, his tone leaving no room to argue back. 'If you do your job properly, you can hit Black and free the boy.'

David reluctantly pulled the rifle that was in his hands up and took aim, trying his best to make sure that the kid wouldn't be hit. He could feel his heart beating in his chest and a cold sweat starting to appear across his body. He knew that he should refuse to do this, but there was something about his boss's stance at the moment that unsettled him. He wasn't usually a religious person but he found himself muttering a small prayer as his finger started to apply pressure to the trigger.

'Please God. Don't let me hurt the kid.'

David fired the weapon and the shot sounded above the traffic that was continuing down the bridge.

James heard the shot but by the time he registered what it was it was too late. He felt the searing pain as the bullet hit him in the upper chest. He felt himself being lifted off his feet by the impact and the feeling of weightlessness as he toppled over the railings. The only thing that he could control was his grip on the boy, which he held on to tight. Seconds later he felt the icy cold water of the choppy and stormy sea below and then his vision was blurred by the water as he sunk down with the boy still in his hands.

Back on top of the bridge Frank turned in the direction of the shot and saw both the sniper and Robert standing back. The sky above them started to release the first drops of rain.

'WHAT THE HELL DO YOU THINK YOU'RE DOING?' Frank shouted, not caring that Robert was his superior anymore. That should not have happened.

THE HARBOUR (SOME DISTANCE FROM THE FORTH ROAD BRIDGE)
SOUTH QUEENSFERRY
18:51

The drops of rain had turned into a proper storm. The rain was falling in sheets to the ground below. The sea crashed against the old stonewalls of the harbour as the storm continued to rage. Wave after wave were hitting the wall, spraying the street above it with salty seawater.

Visible for only a few brief seconds was the shape of something struggling in the stormy waters, before being covered as the next wave rose up and crashed against the harbour wall.

Out of the water, a hand burst forth for a few seconds before being submerged again. Seconds later it surfaced again, this time it tried to grasp the lower rung of a rusty ladder that ran down the harbour wall.

It missed and was soon covered in water again. A moment later it once again reappeared and this time it managed to grab the rung. Another hand reached from the icy blackness of the water, grabbing the rung above it.

Slowly but surely, James pulled himself out of the water. It had taken nearly all of his strength to keep from drowning after he had fallen off of the bridge. Every so often he would feel his strength dying on him and he would be on the verge of giving up but something inside of him wouldn't let that happen and he fought back. The pain in his chest, where the bullet had hit him was almost unbearable, but once again, he wasn't going to lie down and take it. If he was going to die then he would do so fighting back.

About half way up the ladder he was hit by a large wave, slamming him against the ladder and almost causing him to lose his grip. The pain in his chest screamed out from the impact. His vision blurred slightly and had to shake his head to clear it. He began his ascent again.

Reaching the top, he pulled himself over the black railing that ran along the top of the harbour wall. His legs almost buckled on him when he landed on the other side but he was able to keep his balance with a lot of effort. He had to get out of here before the police got this far in their search for him or his body.

He started to look around the street to see if there was anyone there but the storm was keeping the people inside. That was good. No witnesses to see that he was still alive.

He had to leave the area fast and find somewhere where he could hide and recover his strength.

LATE 2002

PULLMAN RESIDENCE

18:44

Frank was back on his feet again. He had been able to get the kitchen knife before James but it didn't seem to make much difference. James still kept coming for him. He swung the knife at the killer again and again. James jumped backwards, but then without warning side stepped and punched Frank hard in the side before he could turn round to face the new threat.

Frank dropped the knife in pain and James kicked it away before he could do anything about it. Lashing out again, James punched Frank in the stomach and then again in the face.

'Time to die Frank,' he said to his badly beaten opponent. James grabbed Frank by the collar of his jacket and threw him up against the wall. Once again punching him in the face after that and then kneeing him in the groin. Frank doubled over in pain, his legs buckling and he collapsed to the floor.

'I'm disappointed, Frank. You've let yourself go. You used to be more of a challenge.'

'You'd be surprised what I can do when I'm ready,' Frank gasped back through his pain. 'I never thought that I'd have to fight you again.'

'Yeah, well. Life's full of surprises,' James retorted before kicking Frank in the stomach.

The sirens of a police car caught James's attention and he stopped what he was doing. He had just gotten out of prison and he was damned if he was going back. He turned back to Frank.

'Saved by the bell,' he said. 'But we will finish this. I promise you.'

Outside of the house the first of the police cars pulled up. This one was unmarked and was driven by John Carter.

2001

James stood outside of Sally Nicholson's new house in Edinburgh itself. He had been plotting his revenge for years, quite content to let the world believe that he was dead but now it was time to come back into the spotlight.

LATE 2002

PULLMAN RESIDENCE

18:45

With one final look at Frank lying in pain on the living room floor, James turned and headed towards the front door.

Outside, John had gotten out of his car and was heading towards the house when the door opened and James left.

'JAMES BLACK,' John shouted. 'HOLD IT RIGHT THERE.'

Instead of obeying James headed right towards John, who tried to back off, but hit the bonnet of his car, stopping him from going any further.

James reached and punched him and then spun him around. Dragging him round to the passenger side of the car, he pulled John's head back and smashed it through the passenger window. The glass shattered and cut into John's face.

John cried out in pain. James pulled John's head back out of the window and reached into the car to find a large shard of glass. Once he had done that he picked it up and after pulling John's head back, exposing his neck, rammed the shard into his jugular. The blood began to spurt out. James glanced up to see three more police cars entering the street.

With no more time he dropped the dying John to the ground and raced around to the driver's side of the car, where he had already observed that the keys were still in the ignition. Starting it up, he turned the car round and sped off in the opposite direction.

Two of the cars gave chase whilst the third pulled up at the body of John and radioed for an ambulance to be sent straight away.

Frank had by this time gotten back to his feet and was leaving the house, in time to see the two police cars giving pursuit. They wouldn't get James that way but at least were trying.

He knew that he was not going to be able to rest until he knew that either James was dead or that he was back in jail, especially now that the killer knew that he was alive. He was going to have to speak to whomever it was he needed to, to get back into the force for the duration of the case, even if it was just as an adviser.

Yet more police cars entered the street and headed in this direction. The police officers on the lawn were asking him who the hell he was and ordering him not to come any closer.

When he didn't listen they warned him that they would use force to stop him if he didn't stop where he was right now. Humouring the police officers, Frank stopped where he was on the lawn. By this time the neighbours were opening their doors to see what all the commotion was about.

The first ambulance arrived in the street and some of the police officers entered the house and came back out pale faced at the sight of the carnage inside. What all of the officers knew but no one wanted to admit was that James Black had escaped again and the death count was going to continue to mount up.

PART 5

LATE 2002

COWGATE AREA

EDINBURGH

22:58

James Black was walking up the street, keeping to the shadows and trying to keep himself to himself for the time being. It had taken him several hours to lose the pursuing police officers after he had left Carl Pullman's place and he wasn't keen in having to start running again. Once he had lost the policemen he had ditched the car that he was driving and had started to walk. Heading towards the city centre because that was the last thing that they would have expected, being as there was still a police presence there after his escape earlier on that day.

He found an abandoned building with the windows boarded up. This would provide shelter for the time being. Making sure that there was no one watching, he moved round to the back of the building and started to pull the boards off of one of the windows, so that he could climb in. Once inside he allowed the board to fall back into place again, shutting out the light almost entirely, but that suited James for the time being.

His mind kept playing over the events of that night. He had gone round to Carl Pullman's house to kill him only to find out that Carl was the copycat killer. As if that hadn't been enough he had also discovered that Frank Thorn was still alive. He'd actually believed that the house fire a year earlier had succeeded in killing Frank, but obviously not.

Now it was time to finish the job. He would have done it tonight, in fact had almost done it tonight but he had been forced to abandon it.

Still it was only a matter of time before he evened up with Frank and this time he wouldn't escape. First though, he had to keep a low profile as the police were pulling out all of the stops to try and find him. When the police numbers started to drop and they had to start pulling the officers onto other cases, then he would start up his killing spree again and Frank would know all about it.

THORN RESIDENCE
12TH FLOOR OF TOWERBLOCK FLATS
SIGHTHILL
EDINBURGH
00:12

Frank closed the front door behind him as he entered his home. He was hoping that his wife Catherine was asleep because what he had to tell her, he wasn't looking forward to at all. He knew however that it would be unlikely as he had left the house nearly six hours earlier and when he had left he had told Catherine that he might have to face James Black again.

As expected, as soon as she had heard the front door close, Catherine appeared in the hallway. Seeing him she ran up to him and embraced him tightly.

'Have you any idea how long you've been away? I've been worried sick,' she said. 'What happened? The news just says that James Black is still on the run. Is that right? He's still out there?'

Frank removed himself from her embrace carefully. As she took a step back and took a closer look at him, she saw the bruises and cuts on his face.

'Oh God,' she muttered. 'What happened?'

'I had another run in with James, that's all. It looks worse than it is. I'll be fine.'

'Tell me what happened,' she pushed.

'Carl's dead,' Frank answered. 'James killed him before I could stop him.'

'That's not your fault,' Catherine replied. 'You did everything that you could.'

'Something else,' Frank said. 'James claimed that Carl was the copy cat killer and upon thinking about it, I think that he might be right.'

Catherine didn't know what to say to this and so remained quiet. Frank readied himself to tell Catherine the rest of the bad news.

'I've spoken to Carl's superior and he's agreed under the extreme circumstances to letting me assist in the case as an advisor.'

Catherine's heart missed a beat and she felt the blood drain from her face.

'No,' she said as she shook her head. 'You can't honestly be thinking of going back. It almost killed you the last time.'

'Catherine,' Frank started. 'I wish there was another way because if there was I'd take it at the drop of a hat, but he knows that I'm alive and he'll keep on coming for me until either, one of us is dead or he's locked up again. The best thing that I can do is to help the police put him behind bars again so that we'll know that it's over once and for all.'

Despite the fact that she didn't like it, Catherine understood that what Frank was saying was the truth. This had to end, one-way or the other. It had dragged on for too long. She nodded to her husband that she understood and headed off towards the bedroom in silence.

THREE WEEKS LATER

SECRET UNDERGROUND INSTALLATION

EDINBURGH

10:02

Raymond Shields entered the boardroom nervously. He had never been inside of this room and had never actually spoken to the main people in the government group that he worked for. He was to all intents and purposes a junior in the group and he had been very surprised to learn that the head of the group was requesting an appointment with him. It was sheer luck that he had stumbled across what he was about to tell the leader.

In the centre of the room, there was a large table around which were seated several high-ranking men in the organisation. Despite their ranks they were all answerable to the elderly man at the head of the table. This wasn't a committee but rather they were here because their work demanded it.

The elderly man leaned forward towards Raymond. 'Mr. Shields,' he said. 'I'm led to believe that you have some very interesting results from your routine work that your section leader asked you to do. Is that right?'

Raymond took a deep breath to calm his nerves and started. 'Yes,' he said. 'I was asked to look into the James Black case as a matter of routine. Our attention was grabbed by the fact that he had survived both a shooting in 1998 and a house fire last year. They should both have killed him, but still he lives, with no scars or anything else that would suggest what he had been through.

'The first thing that I did was to search for all files that I could on him and initially I came up against the same brick wall that the police force did back in the original batch of murders in 1998. There was nothing on him. However as you all know, we have much better resources than the police force does and I was eventually able to find a file on him that had been sealed by International courts since 1973.

'I was able to pull a few strings and the file was opened. The file revealed that during the late sixties through until the early seventies, a Doctor Alan Hilter was conducting genetic experiments years ahead of their time. According to the file he claimed that he was trying to make the perfect human being. Someone with remarkable healing power and completely immune to every possible virus, infection and bacteria on the planet.

'The raw material for these experiments was blood samples that may or may not have been from his patients. That was never established. In late 1971, he got his first real result that we can see - James Black.'

'Hang on a minute,' the elderly man said. 'In fact, back up a minute. I know the name Alan Hilter from somewhere.'

Raymond nodded his agreement. 'Yes you do, but I'm still getting to that part. For reasons unknown to us, Alan gave James up to an adoption agency that re-homed him with the Black's several months later.

'At that point Alan started to work on another child. It was at this time that the law got wind of what he was doing. They shut him down and destroyed the unborn child. In their raid of the doctor's house they found some records that made references to James and they checked up on him. This was mid 1972 by this point.

'Having traced James to his adopted parents, the agencies watched for a few months and did some tests but eventually decided to let him live as he seemed perfectly normal and was in a stable family environment.

'Officially Alan Hilter was found guilty of various crimes and was sentenced to life imprisonment. Unofficially, he was forced to come and work for us in 1973. That is where you know the name from, sir. The group knew that he was done for genetic research and we were interested in his abilities as a scientist. What the group was never made aware of until now was exactly how successful his experiments had been and that the proof of this was still alive. Unfortunately Alan Hilter died several months later in an accident here.

'The file on the case was sealed to protect the identity of James and give him a chance at a normal life. Over the years it has been forgotten. Until now that is. We're still not sure what it was exactly that caused him to turn into a killer, but I believe that Doctor Hilter may have succeeded in his quest to make the perfect human as far as being able to heal himself goes and if that's true then it stands to reason that the part that says that he might be immune to everything else might also be true.'

A man with a large scar running down his left cheek spoke up from the table. 'This is very good work, but I'm puzzled why it is only being done now as opposed to a year ago when it was announced that he had survived the fire in the first place. Surely that would have made more sense. Wouldn't you agree?'

Raymond felt himself flush red with anger at the remark, but held his tongue in check. 'Yes, sir. It would have made much more sense in hindsight, but you've got to remember that like I said it was only just a routine check. We have hundreds of these types of checks every week and they very rarely yield anything useful to the project. We also have a large backlog of these checks and without more man hours or a list of what you would like the section that I work in to prioritise then I'm afraid that these type of delays will happen from time to time.'

Before the scarred man could reply, the elderly man spoke up. 'Thank you Mr. Shields. Excellent work. I'll make sure that you're properly rewarded for your services. That will be all.'

With that Raymond was dismissed from the room. The men around the table remained silent whilst they waited for Raymond to leave and the door to close behind him.

Once Raymond was away, the elderly man addressed the table. 'The real question is: do we really believe that James Black might be immune to as much as our young Mr. Shields would have us believe? And if so then we need to start pulling out the stops to capture him so that we can find out for a fact.'

The table of men all started to talk at once. Each person was trying to voice his or her opinion over everyone else. The elderly man listened to it for a while before reaching his decision.

'Ladies and Gentlemen,' he began. 'I have reached a decision. I think that it is too good an opportunity to pass up without even investigating. I want James Black captured for study and I don't want either the police or the press to get wind of it.'

He turned round to face the scarred man. They didn't really like one and other and the scarred man had made it no secret that he wanted to be in charge of the group and would do everything that he could within the rules to get there. He was however very good at what he did and what he did was to make problems disappear and to ensure that the secrecy of the work was protected.

'I want you in charge of getting hold of him. Do whatever is necessary but get the job done. Is that understood?'

The scarred man nodded his head in agreement. The conversation of how to go about this was brought up.

'How are you going to go about catching him?' one of the younger men at the other end of the table asked.

The scarred man paused for a minute. 'There are various ways to find someone and sooner or later we will find him. First of all, I need to refresh myself with the specifics of the case. Both the original one and the present.'

The elderly man nodded his approval at this and satisfied that if James Black could be caught then he would be, he turned back to the table and started to ask for any other outstanding business.

Once again the table descended into a rabble. Most people at the table wanted to continue talking about what if James Black turned out to be what they hoped he would. The advantages that that would give them against an enemy would be enormous. It was their job after all to protect the British public against all kinds of threats and this was presenting them with an enormous opportunity.

SIX DAYS LATER

CARPENTER RESIDENCE

21:21

James stood in the shadows of Sonya Carpenter's house. He could hear Sonya moving about upstairs. She was just out of the shower and was getting ready for bed now. If only she knew that she had only a short time left on this Earth.

James had waited very patiently for nearly a month. He had watched the press as the stories about him faded from the front-page to no more than a passing comment. Some of the stories had angered him, but he had ignored his impulse to prove to them that he was still to be feared. Some of the latest stories claimed that he had fled from Edinburgh and could now be anywhere in the U.K.

They claimed that if he were still in Edinburgh then wouldn't there have been more murders by now? It seemed to have escaped their attention that he had sometimes went weeks on end without killing anyone during the first investigation. It was nothing more than sensationalism in an effort to sell papers and get viewers to watch T.V.

Now however it was time to show them how wrong they were and get himself more accurate media attention. More importantly, it was time to let Frank know that he wasn't off the hook.

He started to move across the hallway towards the stairs and the sounds of the woman upstairs. He was unarmed as he hadn't yet gotten round to finding a replacement knife for the one that he used to have but that was only a matter of time. Not that he'd need a knife for this. He'd use his bare hands.

In her bedroom at the top of the stairs, Sonya had just finished changing into her nightgown. She left her room to go back to the bathroom as she had forgotten to brush her teeth. Leaving her room, the stairs were situated at her left and the bathroom to her right. She was in an excellent mood as her boyfriend of two years had proposed to her earlier on that day and she'd said yes. It was the happiest day of her life and nothing was going to change that.

She turned right towards her bathroom, singing to herself as she did so. She didn't see the movement from the stairs as James climbed up them. Closer and closer to the top landing he came. He could feel the adrenaline rush through him. He loved this. Reaching the top of the stairs he caught sight of his prey entering the bathroom.

He started to walk towards the bathroom. From within it he could hear the sound of running water and of her brushing her teeth. He smiled to himself. She was all cleaned up for her death. This thought appealed to his sense of humour.

In the bathroom, Sonya finished brushing and put the toothbrush back in the cup holder that she used. She rinsed out her mouth and turned the tap off. She finally saw James, as she turned round to leave the room. All thoughts of marriage went out of her mind as she screamed out in fright and fear.

She recognised her intruder's face from the news several weeks earlier but was not initially able to place it. The look of fear on her face just encouraged James even more, if he even needed any more encouragement.

Lashing out with his fist, he punched Sonya square in the face, sending her staggering backwards. She fell against the bathtub and her legs buckled. Her body fell partially inside of the tub.

James moved across the room fast. He bent down and grabbed her, hauling her to her feet. Meanwhile she was screaming out for help. James had to shut her up because he had to leave his message to Frank and he couldn't risk one of her neighbours hearing the commotion and calling the police and thus interrupting him. He would call the police when he was good and ready.

His mind made up that he had to shut her up, he dragged her over to the sink that she had been brushing her teeth in. Grabbing her hair and pulling her head back, he slammed it forward into the ceramic rim of the sink. The ceramic broke under the impact and there was a loud cracking sound, which James was unsure if it was the sink breaking or Sonya's skull cracking. Either way, Sonya was instantly knocked out.

Throwing her body down to the floor, James turned to the glass shower door on the side of the bath. He moved over to it and smashed his fist into it, causing it to shatter, spraying the bathtub with glass shards. James ignored the small cuts on his hand that this action caused him to receive and bent down into the tub, looking for a suitable glass shard for what he had in mind.

Finding a piece that looked like it would do the job, James turned back to the still unconscious Sonya. The glass in his hand was causing yet another cut in his palm. Once again James ignored it. He had work to do.

POLICE STATION
06:14

Detective Paul Bond moved across the room to meet Frank as he entered. He had just come back from the latest crime scene and had been very surprised when he discovered that no one had called Frank yet. So he had had to do it himself and had spent the last forty odd minutes waiting for Frank to get here.

'He's killed again, hasn't he?' Frank asked.

'Yes,' Paul replied. 'But there's more. Have a look at these.' He handed Frank several photos from the crime scene that he'd only just received himself. He'd had them prioritised.

Frank looked at the pictures of the dead woman. 'What was her name?' he asked.

'Sonya Carpenter,' Paul replied.

'Poor woman,' Frank muttered as he looked through the photos. He stopped at photo of the bathroom wall with a bloody message scrolled on it. The message read: SOON FRANK and was written in what Frank could only assume was the victim's blood.

DOWN THE STREET FROM THE POLICE STATION

SAME TIME

Two men sat inside of an old building across the street and down a bit from the police station. They worked for the scarred man, (who had since returned to the group base) and were monitoring the phone lines in the police station, for anything that might help them to catch James Black. After re-reading the case files, the scarred man had felt that it was a possibility that James would get back in touch with Frank since they still had unfinished business to attend to.

With that in mind, he had arranged for the phone lines in the police station and Frank's home number to be tapped in case James attempted to make contact. He had no idea whether James even knew Frank's home number but it would be easy enough for him to find him at the police station.

It wasn't the only way that the scarred man was pursuing. He had other methods; he just liked to cover all of his bases.

ABANDONED BUILDING

COWGATE AREA

14:41

James sat on the floor of the building that had become his home for the last few weeks. He wouldn't be able to stay here for much longer but it was convenient at the moment.

In front of him lay a mobile phone that he had stolen from his victim the previous night. He was confident that it would still be working fine as there hadn't been anyone to report it as stolen.

He was working out what he would say to Frank in a few minutes when he phoned him at work. He had waited long enough for the message that he had left at the murder scene to reach Frank and he was willing to bet that Frank had seen it by now.

Reaching down, he picked the phone up. He had been very careful not to turn the phone off when he had taken it, as he wasn't sure whether it would ask for a pin number once it was turned back on.

He started to dial the number for the police station that he knew Frank was working in. Once answered, he asked to be transferred to whatever phone extension Frank was working on. Seconds later the phone was answered by Frank and James smiled. It was time for the game to begin.

DOWN THE STREET FROM THE POLICE STATION

SAME TIME

The two men sprung into action when they realised that the man that they were looking for had just phoned in and they started running a trace using state of the art technology that the public didn't even know existed and that the standard military could only dream of.

While one of the two men was running the trace the other was getting on his own phone to report in to his superior.

ABANDONED BUILDING

COWGATE AREA

14:44

James continued to play with Frank as he was guessing that he would be running a trace to try and find his location, but he knew that it took a bit longer to find the location of mobile phone than it did to find a landline.

He taunted Frank with his threats of what he was going to do to his next victim, should Frank not re-capture him by then.

Frank retaliated by shouting back down the phone at him. This brought a smile to James's face. Abruptly the phone that he was using went dead as the battery gave out.

James pulled it away from his ear and looked at it, his mind clicking a second later what had happened. In disgust he threw the phone across the room. It hit the wall and shattered.

'Piece of shit,' he muttered.

POLICE STATION
SAME TIME

Frank pulled the receiver away from his head once it had gone dead. He could feel a sheen of sweat on his forehead. He turned round to the men behind him who had been trying to set up a trace on the phone.

‘Please tell me that we got it,’ said.

The reply was not what he was hoping for and he slammed the phone back down into the cradle in frustration.

SECRET UNDERGROUND INSTALLATION

EDINBURGH

14:50

The scarred man was moving fast down one of the corridors. He had just gotten off the phone with one of his men and they had found the location of James Black due to being able to trace a phone call that he had made to Frank Thorn. The scarred man had suspected that this might happen. Even using their technology, they had barely been able to complete the trace before the connection was lost.

Now he was getting together a group of men that would go in and capture James. He was going to head the operation personally. They would move in fast and hard and they would be gone before the authorities could arrive and do anything about it.

ABANDONED BUILDING
COWGATE AREA

15:27

James sat in the darkness thinking. He could sit like this for hours at a time. His brain mulling over what needed to be done, things he planned to do and how he would do it. In this instance he was thinking about how badly he wanted to make Frank suffer. Frank had been a worthy opponent so far but that didn’t change the fact that he still had to pay for what he had done to James. He would come for Frank soon, but for the moment he would drag it out. He would show Frank that he was helpless to stop him.

Abruptly, there was a cracking sound as one of the boards over the windows was ripped off. James sprung to his feet but was temporarily blinded by torches being shined in his eyes.

Three men entered through the window, each armed with a tranquilliser rifle with a torch attached to the top of the gun so that they could see what they were aiming at. It was these torches that were blinding James.

James snarled and as his eyes quickly adjusted to the lights, he lunged at the intruders. He didn’t even get halfway across the room before three darts hit him in the chest, their contents being injected into his blood stream.

Standing at the window, the scarred man watched as his three hand picked men fired their guns at the killer. His face took on a look of concern when the darts didn't drop James to the floor straight away. Rather the killer continued on towards the men, not even slowing down.

The three men also realising that they were now in danger started to reload more darts into their rifles. They never got the chance. James reached them and grabbed the nearest one. He spun the man round and snapped his neck before turning to face the remaining two.

The tranquilliser drugs were working through his system and his vision began to blur slightly. He began to feel a little lightheaded and stumbled a few steps backwards. Righting himself he managed to focus his eyesight on the two men, in time to see one of them swinging his rifle like a club. The butt of the rifle hit James on the forehead and he fell to the floor.

Meanwhile the other man had reloaded his rifle and took aim again, firing a fourth dart into James's back.

This proved to be too much for even James and his efforts to get back up began to weaken. The man who had clubbed him raised his rifle again and brought it down again - hard.

James's arms gave way and he slumped to his side, his vision turning black as the tranquillisers did their job.

'Well done,' the scarred man congratulated the two surviving men from his team. 'Now pick him up and get him into the back of the van before some do-gooder ends up calling the police at seeing us carrying an unconscious man away against his will.'

The two men did what they were told and started to move the limp form of James out of the window and towards the van.

The public never again heard from James Black, at least not for a long, long time. As the weeks turned into months and finally into years, James was considered as dead by the local history books and although the case was never closed officially, only Frank continued to obsess over it.

What nobody would ever have believed, (not even Frank) was that James would start a chain of events which would bring the Human race down to its knees.

FIVE YEARS LATER

SECRET UNDERGROUND INSTALLATION

EDINBURGH

12:00

The elderly man stood in a darkened room looking through a one-way mirror at the occupant in the next-door room. James Black sat in a chair on the other side of the mirror. He was dressed in clinical white trousers and t-shirt. His arms and legs were shackled with re-enforced metal cuffs.

The group had learned very fast that the cuffs and shackles were necessary. They had intended to keep him drugged up after they had gotten him but his immune system had built up a very good immunity to the tranquilliser that they were using and within days it was completely useless. This mistake had cost them the lives of three scientists before they had gotten him with a new tranquilliser that had rendered him unconscious again. Slowly but surely however, he had become immune to nearly every one of the tranquillisers that the group had. They only had a few different types left and they were going to use one of them here today and just had to hope that this wasn't the day that it stopped working.

After the escape incident it had been decided that he had to be restrained at all times and the shackles were brought in.

That had been the only incident in the last five years however and the group had been able to reap some of the rewards that justified the risk that they had taken to capture him. It turns out that Raymond Shields's file on James had been accurate and James seemed to be able to shake off everything that they threw at him. Sometimes it took days and other times it took weeks and weeks.

They had started off with small viruses and infections and over the years they had increased the intensity of what they were exposing him to. So far he had provided them with the groundwork for cures for nearly every type of Cancer, the HIV/AIDS virus and a genetically modified Small Pox virus that had been developed by the military for use during any future conflicts. These were just some of the main ones that he had been exposed to.

Today however was the day that they were going to test the mother of all viruses. This was the one that they had been building up to over the last five years. Everything that they hoped to achieve rested on this test. The experiment would begin in a few minutes.

The door to the room opened and the scarred man entered. The two men still didn't see eye to eye but there was a level of professional respect between them that had grown slightly over the years.

'We're ready to begin,' the scarred man reported. He had taken on the whole project concerning James Black and usually supervised the tests himself. This was different though. Usually the elderly man didn't come to watch. It was because of the virus that they were going to be using today that he had turned up to observe.

It was hard to get hold of live samples of this particular virus and the only man in the group with the authority to release stocks for tests was the elderly man.

The elderly man turned to look at the scarred man and nodded his go-ahead. The scarred man turned without another word and left the room again. The elderly man turned back to watching James in the next-door room. For a brief second it seemed that their eyes met and the elderly man felt a chill run down his spine.

'He knows I'm here,' the elderly man muttered to himself, even as his logic told him that this couldn't be so. James couldn't see through the glass, not as this distance surely?

Inside of the room, James narrowed his eyes as he focused on the mirror. He wasn't stupid. He knew that there had to be someone on the other side of the mirror. He just wasn't sure whom. He wasn't even sure who these people were and where he was anymore. He had no idea how much time had passed since his capture or what had been happening in the outside world. He tensed his muscles in the chair against the cuffs that held him in place. It was time that he was getting out of here. He had tried once before, shortly after his capture but hadn't lasted long before being caught again. He had been biding his time very patiently waiting for the right time to present itself for his escape. Always ready and always waiting, his time would come again and if they followed the same procedure that they usually did, he hoped that it would be here and now.

There was a hissing sound as the vents in the corners of the room began to open and release a gas into the room. James felt his body begin to weaken as he had done the last two times that they had used this method to subdue him. But he knew that was all that would happen. The concentration of the gas wasn't strong enough anymore to knock him out. They didn't know that yet however. They would soon enough though, he thought to himself.

He allowed his body to slump in the chair and his head to fall against his chest, creating the impression that he was out for the count.

The elderly man watched all of this with a cold impartial face. He waited for a few more minutes before moving across the room towards a telephone and picking up the receiver.

'Move on to phase two,' he ordered, before hanging up. He turned his attention back to the room where James sat slumped in the chair. Once the gas had been dispersed from the room, he watched as four men entered and approached James. The men were in airtight quarantine suits and were pushing a stretcher in front of them.

The tallest of the four men reached James and produced a set of keys so that he could begin to unlock the prisoner's shackles.

James felt the cuffs being removed followed seconds later by a sense of weightlessness as he was picked up and moved onto the stretcher. Although he was conscious, he was still slightly weak from the gas. Another few minutes and he should be feeling fine again. So he kept up the charade of being knocked out.

Once he was on the stretcher, he felt his arms and legs being secured again with material straps. He wasn't too bothered by this, as he knew that they wouldn't hold up to his strength, like the metal ones did. Seconds later he felt movement as the stretcher was pushed out of the room towards his destination. James could feel his concentration and focus sharpening again. Nearly time.

The elderly man watched as James was moved from the room and once gone from view he left his room and entered the corridor, where he ran into the scarred man, who was now dressed in a quarantine suit of his own, a small medical case held in his right hand. Further down the corridor, the four men continued to push James towards his destination. The elderly man and the scarred man gave a brief nod to one and other before the scarred man passed his superior and followed the other men down the corridor.

The scarred man caught up with the four men and the stretcher as they rounded a corridor and came to a halt at a large metal airtight door, with a glowing red keypad to the right of it.

The scarred man moved up to the keypad and entered an eight-digit code. A second later there was a hissing sound and the doorway began to slide open. Inside was an airlock with another heavy airtight door on the other side of it. The second door was still closed. Like the first door, there was a keypad next to that as well.

The group of men entered the airlock, pushing James in front of them. Once all of them were inside, the scarred man moved over to the secondary keypad and entered another eight-digit code. The door that they had just entered started to slide close. Once closed the men were momentarily trapped between the two closed doors but a moment later, the second door started to open.

The room on the other side of the door was sterile white and bare of any furnishings with the exception of a small stainless steel table. The far wall of the room was comprised of re-enforced glass from which the members of the group could watch whatever was happening inside of the room. Today the only occupant was the elderly man. He had come down the corridor watching the group of five men and James as they entered the quarantine room. Then he had let himself into the viewing room, to watch the administration of the virus. He was very nervous about something going wrong. The virus they were using was very dangerous if not used correctly and he didn't want any screw-ups.

James was pushed into the room and the stretcher placed next to the table. The scarred man motioned for the other four men to leave. They did so gladly. Once they were gone the inner door closed locking the scarred man in alone with James who was still faking unconsciousness.

The scarred man moved towards the table and placed the medical case on top of it. Opening it up, he revealed a single syringe. Inside of this syringe was the isolated virus, for which the group had spent decades, trying to find a cure for and still no success. This virus had the potential to destroy mankind once and for all, which was why the group were so desperate to find a cure.

The scarred man had wanted to try the virus on James, years earlier but had been told that they needed to work their way up to it, after all what if it was the one to kill him. They would have nothing to show for their efforts, at least this way they had had a lot of positive results from him.

The scarred man picked up the syringe and turned back to James. He reached out and twisted the killer's right arm so that he could inject the virus into his system.

James felt his arm being moved and knew that it was now or never. He tensed his left arm and got ready to make a large effort so that he could not only break the strap but also inflict damage to the man next to him.

The scarred man placed the point of the needle against James's arm, resting it on a vein and was about to push it in when the killer's eyes snapped open. He barely had time to respond to this before James wrenched his left arm upwards ripping the strap out of its fitting on the side of the stretcher. His fist continued upwards and connected with the scarred man's jaw.

The scarred man stumbled back from the impact of the blow, the syringe falling to the floor. Instantly James was reaching out with his free hand to undo the strap holding his other hand down. This was followed by him leaning forward to remove the straps holding his ankles. As he was doing this he was scanning the room for a weapon. The only thing that he saw was the syringe lying on the ground. He lunged for it.

Meanwhile, the scarred man had already made his way over to the door. The experiment had gone wrong and he needed to escape before it got out of hand. He keyed his code into the inner keypad and the door opened. Stumbling into the airlock, he raced over to the outer door. He keyed his code into this door and heard the inner door close behind him. He breathed a sigh of relief at this, which was cut short by a hand grabbing him by the shoulder and spinning him round. He hadn't been quick enough. James had gotten through. With the inner door closed the outer door begun to open allowing James access into the main hallways of the installation.

'You're coming with me,' James muttered to his hostage, the syringe held tightly in his right hand.

The outer door finished opening to reveal six men dressed in black uniforms and armed with tranquilliser guns. They were also armed with real guns in holsters too. Behind the six men stood the elderly man who had ordered that the men be scrambled as soon as he saw that James wasn't under the effect of the knock out gas.

Without even thinking about it, James swung the scarred man in front of him and pushed the point of the syringe through his quarantine suit, so that the needle rested against his hostage's neck.

'DROP YOUR WEAPONS,' James shouted at the guards. There was no response. Instead the men took a step forward.

'I HAVE NO IDEA WHATS IN THIS SYRINGE BUT IF YOU DON'T WANT TO RISK EXPOSURE THEN YOU WILL DROP YOUR WEAPONS NOW.'

'The virus that you hold in your hands is not an airborne one,' the elderly man replied calmly. 'If you inject him, then we will all be quite alright for the time being.'

James considered this for a second, his brain running everything through as quickly as it could. He shook his head. 'If that's true then why is he wearing this suit?'

The elderly man smiled at this. 'Nothing more than an extra precaution. No harm in that, is there?'

James didn't reply to this but instead started to edge along the corridor keeping his hostage in front of him as a shield. The guards continued to keep their weapons aimed at him, waiting for the order to fire.

The scarred man could feel himself sweating as he felt the point of the needle press against his neck.

'We both know that those tranquilliser guns that your men are using will probably be useless against me and that I could just as easily get past them to you. Maybe you'd be more cooperative if it was your life on the line,' James stated.

The elderly man thought about what James had just said. 'No you're not going anywhere,' he replied. 'That virus will not leave this installation. We will kill you if we have to.'

'After all the trouble that you've gone to capture and keep me here?' James retorted sarcastically. 'I don't think so.'

'Do you really want to test me?' the elderly man asked.

James could see more guards moving down the corridor towards him. 'I grow impatient with this. If you don't want me to kill this man, then you will order your men to drop their weapons and you will help me to get out. I'll even return your precious virus once I'm out.'

'I'll kill him also before I let you out,' the elderly man replied.

James looked at the elderly man, their eyes locking. That statement drilled home the realisation that his opponent was as ruthless as he was. 'You know something?' James asked. 'I actually believe you.'

Without warning, he pulled the syringe back out of the scarred man's suit and threw him into the six closest guards, knocking four of them over. Some of the guards fired off their guns at the exposed target, but none hit him as he moved fast towards the elderly man.

The elderly man barely had time to register this before James had reached him and grabbed him, twisting him round, so that he was now the human shield. The needle of the syringe was pushed against the elderly man's neck.

'I REPEAT THE ORDER,' James shouted at the guards who were closing in. 'DROP YOUR WEAPONS.'

By this time the scarred man was back on his feet and had ripped off the facemask of his suit, glaring at his attacker. Still the guards didn't drop their weapons.

James moved his mouth close to the elderly man's ear. 'Order them to drop their weapons or I will inject you with this stuff.'

The elderly man knew that he should refuse for the greater good of the country, after all he couldn't allow the virus to escape, but now that it was his life on the line and not someone else's it was a different story.

'Lower your weapons,' he eventually ordered the guards.

'Sir?' the lead guard questioned.

'DO IT,' the elderly man ordered.

'NOBODY DO ANYTHING,' the scarred man shouted, turning to face the elderly man as he did so. 'Nothing personal Sir, but you're not in a position to make a sound neutral decision at the moment.'

The guards were now caught between conflicting orders from the two highest-ranking people in the group. They were very unsure of what to do.

'You will get them to drop their weapons and you will help me to get out of this building or I promise you, you'll regret it,' James whispered into the elderly man's ear.

'Read your organisation charter,' the elderly man said to both the scarred man and the guards. 'It clearly says that the head of the group has sweeping authority with no exceptions. That is why the group is careful whom it elects. With that in mind I'm ordering you to drop your weapons. Failure to do so is the same as treason.'

The guards hesitated for a few more seconds before finally lowering their weapons.

'Well done,' James muttered. 'Now help me to get out of here, right now.'

'If I do that, can I have your word that you'll return the syringe to me once you're out?'

'Done,' James replied. 'But be warned any tricks and you will regret it.'

The two men started to move down the corridor, James following the elderly man's directions as to where the exit was. The scarred man watched them leave and started to follow at a distance.

James and the elderly man had to stop several times to tell new groups of guards to back down and drop their weapons, but slowly and surely they made their way up towards the surface. James could see the scarred man following but wasn't too bothered by this, as long as he kept to the distance. Behind him there were some guards, but they were staying even further away as they had been ordered to.

Minutes later, they emerged into the daylight. The sky was grey and overcast but still never the less daylight. The alleyway they had entered was empty with metal gates up at either end.

'Do you have a car?' James asked his hostage.

'Yes,' the elderly man replied. 'It's over in this direction.'

The elderly man and James headed down the alley. Through the metal gates and onto a main street, with people on it. They were unfortunately drawing attention to themselves. The scarred man continued to follow, entering the alley from the installation, he was damned if he was going to let James get away.

James and the elderly man had reached the car and the elderly man was unlocking the driver's door for him, before handing him the keys.

James pulled the needle away from the elderly man's neck and whilst still holding on to him with his left hand, leaned into the car to check whether there was any traps or surprises waiting for him.

Across the street, the scarred man saw this as his chance. He raced across the road and before the elderly man could order him to stop, had reached James and punched him hard in the kidney.

James lurched forward in the car, the syringe falling from his hand to the bottom of the foot well inside, beside the pedals.

'NO,' the elderly man called out. It was all going to hell.

James pulled himself back out of the car and stood upright to his full height. The scarred man took another swing at him, but this time James was ready. He caught the scarred man's fist mid-swing and twisted his arm round, forcing the scarred man to face away from him. With no other effort, he shoved the scarred man's head through the back passenger side window. The glass shattered and the shards started to cut into the scarred man's face, spraying a fine mist of blood onto the back passenger seat.

There were screams from passers-by and the attention that they had been drawing to themselves turned into calls for the police to be called.

James pulled the scarred man back out of the broken window and shoved him down to the pavement.

'Tell him that he's lucky to be alive,' James snapped at the elderly man, before he climbed into the car and started the engine. Seconds later he was driving away from the scene.

The elderly man got down to his knees to help the scarred man back to his feet. They had to get out of here before the police came here. This would risk too much exposure to their group. Yes they had people in the police who did stuff for them but the last thing he needed at the moment was exposure. He caught one last glimpse of his car along with James and the syringe disappearing into the distance.

THORN RESIDENCE

12TH FLOOR OF TOWERBLOCK FLATS

SIGHTHILL

EDINBURGH

01:53

Frank Thorn woke up with a jolt. He was covered in sweat and his heart was thumping heavily in his chest. He turned to make sure that he hadn't woken Catherine up. She was still sleeping peacefully by his side.

He slid out of bed and made his way to the bathroom at the end of the hall. Turning on the overhead light, he moved over to the sink to splash water on his face. Glancing at his watch, he turned the tap back off and began to head back to bed. He had an early start tomorrow.

He was back in the police force properly. He wasn't as respected as he used to be but was still a detective never the less. Five years earlier when James Black had just disappeared, he had insisted that they kept the case open, which they did but it was now generally considered that James was dead or why had he stopped killing for all of this time?

Frank on the other hand insisted that until they had a body, they had to assume that he was still alive. His fear that James was still alive and that this wasn't really over had prompted him to continue his return from retirement and over the years he gathered a reputation as a man obsessed by this one case. He still worked on other cases but he was always on the lookout for anything that might explain what had happened to James back in 2002. He had to know for sure so that he could have peace of mind once and for all.

Catherine was the only one who understood the importance of why he had to do this. If he failed then, her life might be in danger as well. He got back into bed, to try and get some sleep before he had to get back up again.

MEDICAL WARD

SECRET UNDERGROUND INSTALLATION

EDINBURGH

02:13

The scarred man opened the one eye that he still had. One of the pieces of glass from the car window had punctured his right eye and there was currently a piece of gauze over it. His face hurt like hell, stinging from the various cuts that the glass had made.

The door to the room opened and the elderly man entered. He had been watching on the security camera for when the scarred man would wake up from the anaesthetic that had been used on him whilst the doctors had worked on his face and eye.

'I hope you're proud of yourself,' the elderly man stated coldly.

'What are you talking about?' the scarred man asked.

'Thanks to you, we not only lost James but he still has the syringe with the virus.'

'You're the one who ordered the guards away and helped him get out,' the scarred man countered angrily.

The elderly man took a deep breath to keep calm. 'We'd lost James anyway, with or without the guards. He was either going to get away or we were going to have to kill him. That wasn't the object though. The object was getting the syringe back before he could do any damage with it. I, at least, had arranged for the syringe to be returned to us upon his escape.'

'Did you really think that James would hand over the virus once he'd gotten away?'

'Yes, I do,' the elderly man replied. 'James may be a lot of things but there is nothing in any of the case files that would suggest that he was a liar. I feel that he would have given me the syringe once he was about to leave, had you not intervened, that is.'

The scarred man had to bite his tongue before he said something that he was going to regret.

'If James releases that virus, I will make sure that you are held accountable for it. Do I make myself clear?'

The scarred man nodded his head in reply. He knew that if he tried to say something then he would end up losing the plot. He watched as the elderly man left the room, his rage eating away at him. He would re-capture James again and he would secure the syringe with the virus inside of it. He would do all of this personally.

TWO DAYS LATER

22:03

James sat in the driver's seat of a rusting red car. He'd dumped the elderly man's car several hours after he had taken it. He knew that they would be looking for it. He was now taking another car every day at the moment to reduce the risk of getting caught. He was trying to take the older models that no one would give a second look at.

Over the last few days he'd been trying to find out everything that he had missed over the last five years. He'd looked up himself in the local history books and discovered that he was considered dead by many, which was something that he was going to do something about later on tonight.

The history books also revealed several other items of mild interest to him. It would appear that in late 2003 a terrorist bomb went off on the Forth Road Bridge rendering it unsafe for people to use. Part of the bridge still stood on the Edinburgh side but it was gradually falling to pieces.

He'd continued to read the article to discover that a new bridge had begun being built three years later and that the cars had to use a ferry system if they wanted over the Firth of Forth.

He closed his eyes and his mind wandered back to that fateful evening back in 1998. He remembered himself holding the young boy hostage, the bullet hitting him in the chest and then falling over the railing into the sea below.

He'd also tried finding out anything about Frank that he could. He hadn't forgotten about him after all of these years. This puzzled him slightly as he had assumed that it was just a phase all those years ago. If Frank were still alive and living in Edinburgh then he would get the message after what James was planning to do tonight.

On the passenger seat he had a sheathed knife like he used to use. He had stolen it out of a Military and Camping store. Beside the knife lay the syringe that he had found lying in the foot well before he ditched the elderly man's car. He didn't know what was in it, but he did know that it was important to some people, so he kept it. You never know. It might come in handy.

With that, he started the engine and headed off to do what he did best.

POLICE STATION

22:07

Detective Michelle Gibson stood up from her desk. She was getting ready to go home. She was only here this late because she and her new partner Frank Thorn had a small mountain of paper work to plough through.

She could see Frank heading back towards the desk that they were at. He had a plastic cup of coffee in his hands. She had only just recently been paired with him over the last few weeks and wasn't yet sure what to make of him.

She'd been looking forward to working with him. She'd heard all about him. Who hadn't? The only man to go head to head with Edinburgh's most notorious serial killer, James Black, and survive to tell the tale.

His reputation was slightly tarnished now as a man obsessed with the case, unable to let it go. So far she'd seen no sign of this though.

'Calling it a night?' Frank asked her as he approached.

She nodded her head in agreement. 'Had enough for one night. Why don't you call it a draw as well? Head home to your wife.'

'I'll be leaving in the next fifteen, twenty minutes. I just want to finish up first.'

Michelle smiled and put her jacket on. 'I guess I'll see you tomorrow then,' she said before leaving him to it.

CITY HOSPITAL

22:20

James entered the hospital without anyone noticing. He blended in. he was dressed in black and wearing a long white coat with a false I.D. tag on the pocket. The tag wouldn't stand up to close inspection but then no one was interested in him. They each had their own problems and didn't care about anyone else's. He was wearing the sheathed knife on his belt but the coat that he was wearing hid it. The syringe lay inside of the coat pocket.

He glanced at the floor plan that was displayed on the back wall. It didn't take him long to find what he was looking for, the children's wards.

He began to work his way through the hospital up several flights of stairs towards his destination. The only person that he encountered was a night janitor and he didn't even give him a second glance. The I.D. tag seemed to work.

Reaching his destination, he had a quick look around the ward. There was no doctors or nurses around but there was small red call buttons beside each bed should one of the occupants need assistance.

He moved through to another part of the ward. This particular part only had six children sleeping in it. The lights in the ward were dimmed so as to aid their sleep. Two of the children had their legs in plaster casts, another was hooked up to a drip and the other three didn't seem to have anything wrong on the surface, not that James could see anyway. Not that any of that mattered to the killer.

James moved over to the kid with the drip and picked up his chart. The name read Sean. No surname, but that wasn't important. He walked over to one of the empty beds and started to pull the pillowcases off of all three pillows that sat on top. Walking back over to Sean, he dropped the pillowcases at the end of his bed. He would need them in a few minutes. Before he started he glanced around to make sure that there was still no one about. Once satisfied, he reached out and grabbed hold of the plastic tube of the drip.

Pulling the knife out from its sheath, he sliced through the tube. The contents started to drip down onto the floor from the top end. The end of the tubing that was still stuck in the back of Sean's hand began to turn red as his blood began to fill the void that the fluid in the drip had previously been filling. The blood reached the cut part of the tube and started to drip down onto the floor. Slowly, but surely, creating a puddle.

POLICE STATION

22:25

Frank turned his computer off and grabbed his jacket. It was time to go home. He had had enough as well.

CITY HOSPITAL

22:30

James stood back, watching as the puddle of blood continued to expand onto the floor. The dim lighting above was reflected by the crimson puddle. He had rammed one of the pillowcases into Sean's mouth to stop him calling out when he inevitably woke up. He had woken up at this and started to panic. This had caused his heart to speed up and the flow of blood leaving his body increased. Then James had knocked him out with one good punch. The blood continued to flow onto the floor.

He picked up the two remaining pillowcases and moved onto the next bed. This one contained a young girl. He checked the name on this bed. She was called Anne. She'd fallen asleep listening to her portable CD player, which was sitting on the bed beside her. He moved to the side of the bed and being careful not to make any unnecessary sounds, pulled open her mouth and rammed one of the pillowcases inside to muffle her cries for help.

Anne woke up and started to struggle, causing James to have to hold her in place with his left arm. With his right hand, James pulled back the sheet that covered her up and reached down to his belt to get his knife again.

Anne's struggles knocked her CD player off the side of the bed and it hit the floor with a clatter, waking the occupant of the next bed.

James raised the knife above Anne's chest with the intention of bringing it down hard and killing her, but he stopped when he heard the scream of the young girl next to Anne who had just woken up.

He snapped his head round towards the source of the scream. Rage soaring through him at the thought of his plans being ruined by a mere child. He considered just killing the screaming girl but the damage was already done. The rest of the ward was awake and shouting for help and pressing their call buttons. Those that could get out of bed did so and started to back as far away from the intruder as they could.

'HEY YOU,' someone shouted out.

James turned to face the owner of the new voice. It came from a doctor who had entered the ward with two nurses, to see what all of the commotion was about. With a snarl of rage, James released Anne and lunged at the new arrivals. He shoulder barged his way past them and started to run down hallway to the stairs.

22:33

Frank was in his car driving home. He had his portable police radio on the passenger seat as he always did, just in case. It was on and he was half listening to what was being said. There wasn't anything really serious happening at the moment. No sooner had he thought that when he heard the call for all police units in the area of the city hospital to report there, asap as there had been a serious disturbance, involving a murder. He wasn't really in the vicinity and he wasn't even on duty, but something about this was niggling him. He wanted to go home but he had to check this out. It was if he was drawn to the incident.

With his mind made up to at least take a look; he swerved his car down a side alley to take a short cut towards the hospital. He could be there in about fifteen minutes traffic permitting. He started to increase his speed, once again unable to say why he was desperate to get there.

CITY HOSPITAL

22:40

James reached the ground floor and began to make his way towards the exit. He turned the corner and slid to halt. Three large security guards stood at the exit, not letting anyone out. The hospital had locked down in an effort to keep him here until the main police force arrived presumably.

James was stunned. Security had tightened greatly since 2002. Never the less, he was leaving and he was going to do it now. He walked purposely over to the guards. Seeing him, they closed ranks at the entrance way.

'Sorry, sir. No one leaves here at the moment until the police arrive. We have a situation inside,' the lead guard said, completely unaware that he was talking to the cause of the incident

'Get out of my way, if you want to live,' James replied simply.

The three guards glanced at one and other. Each starting to think the same thought, that this was the man that they were trying to keep inside.

James reached down to his belt to get his knife again, but the guards saw this and reacted quickly. 'Take him down,' the largest guard ordered.

The two flanking guards lunged. James ducked a large fist, threw himself to the ground and swept out with his feet as he did so. The closest guard had his feet taken out from underneath him and he fell to the ground. James could hear the sound of police sirens in the distance. He pulled the knife out fully and plunged it into the guard's chest. There was a cracking sound as he did and the blade grated against the bone. A few drops of blood sprayed upwards onto James's face.

James didn't have time to pull the knife back out before one of the other security guards grabbed him from behind, clamping his large arms around James in a bear hug so that the killer couldn't move his hands as freely. The guard hauled James back to his feet, all the while keeping him in the grip.

The third guard moved forward to James and lashed out, punching him in the face. Despite the bear hug, James began to manoeuvre his hand into the coat pocket, his fingers feeling for and eventually finding what he was looking for. Meanwhile the third guard leaned in close to James in an effort to appear menacing.

'You're wasting your time trying to struggle,' the guard said as he leaned in.

James seized the opportunity and like lightening moved his head forward, his mouth open. His teeth clamped onto the guard's cheek, before the guard could pull back in time. He squeezed tight and felt the coppery taste of blood enter his mouth. The guard screamed in pain. James started to move his teeth in a sideways sawing motion. This caused his teeth to cut through more muscle and flesh. The guard pulled back altogether, but James refused to release his grip and there was a tearing sound as a portion of the guard's cheek was ripped off altogether. Blood was beginning to drip from the wound onto the floor, mixing with the expanding pool of blood from the now dead guard on the floor, the knife still sticking out from his chest.

The third guard began lashing out at James in retaliation at what the killer had just done to his face, but his aim was clouded with pain and anger. James snapped his head sideways in an effort to avoid the blows, exposing the guard behind him to the attacks. The guard holding James twisted his head also in an effort to avoid the blows that his colleague was making. Having to do this resulted in his grip on James loosening slightly.

With more freedom to move, the killer wrenched his right hand free of the bear grip, pulling the syringe out of his pocket as he did so. At the same time he threw his head backwards so that it hit the guard holding him square in the face. The surprise of this caused the guard holding him to release his grip fully.

With his left hand, James punched the guard in front of him hard in the face. The impact of the punch coupled with the pain of what James had already done to his face caused to guard to collapse to the ground.

Spinning round, James swung the syringe in an arc at the guard that had been holding him. It stabbed into the guard's shoulder and James pushed the plunger all the way down.

He had hoped for some sort of instant reaction, but no such luck. The guard looked down at the syringe and pulled it out again before lunging at James. The killer, ready this time, met the lunge and threw the guard down to the ground, moving in to finish him off.

By this time the fight in the hallway had attracted the attention of numerous people and more guards. The first of the police cars were also pulling up outside of the hospital.

Despite his desire to kill this man, he had to go. James reached down and grabbed his knife from the body of the dead guard, before he turned and ran out of the exit. He had to find a car somewhere and make his escape.

The guard that he'd thrown down to the ground scrambled back to his feet and followed suit. He was going to get this man. It had turned personal now. James bolted past the first of the police cars before they even knew what was happening and the guard followed. By the time they had gotten out of their cars and had reported it the two figures were lost in the distance.

James continued to twist and turn down street after street slowly but surely making his escape. The guard behind him was starting to feel unwell. He could feel himself starting to burn up. His head was thumping. What had been in that syringe that this bastard had injected him with?

He suddenly stopped giving chase. He had to rest for five minutes. He leaned against the wall of a building and let himself start to slide down it.

SAME TIME

Frank wasn't far away from the hospital and getting closer all of the time. The street that he was on was quiet at this time of night and he slowed down to take a tight corner.

A figure in a white coat flashed out in front of him. Frank hit the brakes but it was too late. The car hit the man, throwing him up onto the bonnet and into the windshield, causing it to crack. The man rolled back off of the bonnet and fell to the ground.

Frank got out of the car to see if the man was okay and to offer help, but the man was already back on his feet, with his back to him. Frank noticed bloodstains on the white coat.

'Are you alright?' he asked.

James had been about to run off again. He didn't have time for any more distractions but as soon as he heard the voice he paused. He turned round to face Frank and for the first time in five years the two of them locked eyes with one and other.

Frank felt the blood start to drain from his face. His worst fear confirmed. James Black was alive, well and still in Edinburgh.

Frank made the first move, by diving back into his car and grabbing for the glove compartment for the gun that he kept there. He pulled it out and swung it round to take aim but James had already gone, disappeared into the night.

23:11

The security guard stumbled across the road, not sure where he was going, just knowing that he had to keep moving. If he stopped again, he was afraid that he wouldn't get back up. He had intended to go back to the hospital to get treatment but he wasn't even sure where he was anymore. He couldn't concentrate at the moment and his body felt as if it was on fire, his throat was dry and he couldn't speak as a result.

Deep down the guard suspected that this was the end for him, but he didn't want to face that just yet and so he continued to wander around aimlessly hoping against hope that he would find his way back to the hospital.

SECRET UNDERGROUND INSTALLATION

EDINBURGH

00:34

The group members gathered around the table. Various conversations were being spoken at the same time and they were all wondering why they had been called out at such a late hour.

The door to the room opened and the elderly man entered. He moved to the head of the table and took a seat.

'Ladies and gentlemen,' he started. 'Thank you all for coming out at such short notice. I've called you here to inform you that earlier on tonight serial killer James Black released one of our most dangerous viruses whilst inside of a hospital.'

'Which virus?' one of the group asked.

The elderly man fired him a look before answering. 'The virus,' he said. He didn't need to be any more specific than that.

'The hospital has been quarantined by the Military Police and we are testing everyone inside for signs of infection. All dead bodies are being destroyed but we are still having problems locating the guard who was actually infected with the virus. The only reason that we know it has been released is from the testimony of another one of the guards who tried to stop James and now has a chunk missing from his face.'

'So is there any point in this quarantine, if the man that is infected isn't in it?'

'It is a precaution,' the elderly man answered.

'If the virus gets out, what can we do about it?'

'We have every reason to believe that James Black would be immune to the virus. Now, more than ever before we must re-capture him, so that we can expose him to the virus and hopefully find out how his body fights it.

That is our only hope of a cure and since its starting to look unlikely that we're going to find the guard in time to stop the virus from spreading then we're going to need James alive.'

Once again the various conversations started, as everyone tried to speak at once. The elderly man picked up some of what was being said.

'...the hell are we going to get him alive?'

'...been prevented.'

'...never have happened.'

Suddenly another voice rose above the rest. Everyone stopped talking and turned round to face the owner of the voice. The scarred man stood in the doorway. His right eye was still covered by a gauze patch. He waited until he was sure that he had everyone else's attention.

'I'll catch him alive,' he said. 'I caught him the last time. I can catch him again.'

The elderly man shook his head. 'No. You're too involved now. I can't have you trying to settle a score with him. This is too important.'

The scarred man turned to face the elderly man. 'You know that I'm the best person to catch him. That's why you asked me five years ago and as you already pointed out. Our time is running out. We have to act before the virus spreads. We have to get James fast and I can do that.'

The elderly man paused to think about what had just been said. Although he didn't like it, the scarred man's argument made sense. Eventually he nodded his approval.

'I don't care what it takes, but I want him alive,' he ordered.

'We have to find him first,' a young man from the table shouted out.

The scarred man turned to face the owner of the voice. 'Five years ago James seemed very drawn to Detective Frank Thorn. It was this that allowed us to catch him the first time. We also know from our source in the police force that Frank and James ran into each other as he was escaping. James got away but it is very probable that he will contact Frank again. Amongst other things I want Frank's numbers tapped again. Both his home and his work numbers. James doesn't know that that was what got him caught in the first place and probably won't think twice about phoning him.'

The elderly man nodded to the scarred man before getting up and walking out of the room. He had a feeling of dread hanging over him. He knew that time was running out to catch James and that the consequences of not catching him would be unthinkable. He remained however, sceptical about whether they would be able to capture James again. Despite what the scarred man had said about James not clicking that the phones were tapped five years earlier, he felt that it wouldn't take him long to work it out if he'd thought about it. And over the last five years he'd had a lot of time to think. He sighed. He'd just have to wait and see.

POLICE STATION

10:23

Frank stormed down the corridor, his temper starting to get the better of him. He'd spent all morning in the office with his superiors trying to get them to really listen to him when he said that James Black was still alive and that he wasn't just ranting. Although the Black case had never been closed, they were all still very sceptical. They said they believed him but that was just to humour him.

Their attention was more focused on the Military presence in the city that had appeared without any warning. They were quarantining the hospital that James had been in and the radius of the quarantine was expanding slowly as the day wore on. They wouldn't or couldn't say where the orders to do this came from and they wouldn't let any of the police force into the crime scene, supposedly for their own safety.

He reached and entered his office, slamming the door behind him. The glass pane rattled in the frame with the impact.

'That's nice,' Michelle Gibson commented from her desk in the corner of the room. Frank spun round at the sound of her voice.

'I thought I gave you a job to do,' he snapped.

Michelle felt her own temper start to flare up at the way with which had just spoken to her as if she were less than him. 'We can't get the security tapes from the hospital because we can't find out who's in charge of this quarantine thing…'

Before she could continue, Frank cut in. 'I need those tapes to prove to these assholes in charge that James is still alive.'

He turned to walk out of his office and Michelle started to follow. 'OK,' she said. 'Assuming that you're right and that you didn't make a mistake why has James waited all these years before he started to kill again?'

Frank spun back round to face her again, his temper no longer held in check. 'First of all, I didn't make a mistake. James Black is alive,' he hissed at her. 'And secondly he waited three years after falling off the road bridge before he picked up where he left off the last time. This time he's waited five. I'm sure that he's got his reasons but we'll never know them. Now will you just do what you're told?'

With that, he turned and walked back out of the office again, leaving Michelle to her thoughts.

THREE DAYS LATER

FORD RESIDENCE

21:03

James sat calmly in the living room of this house, collecting his thoughts and running through his mental notes about what he needed to do. He'd broken into this house early on in the day and had killed the lone owner. A man named Mr. Jack Ford was lying dead on the living room carpet, his neck broken.

He'd been rigging the house all day against anyone entering against his will. He didn't know who the group of men who'd held him for five years were but he felt that it was safe to assume that they'd be looking for him. He'd seen the news about the hospital quarantine and he knew that it was connected to the syringe that he'd used. It would then stand to reason that they'd be looking for him if for no other reason than to make sure that he didn't expose them. Even if they weren't looking for him, it was better safe than sorry.

He turned his mind back to his personal agenda and decided that it was time to have some fun.

Getting up, he walked through to the hallway where Mr. Ford kept his main house phone. He picked up the receiver and started to dial. Seconds later the phone at the other end started to ring. He didn't have long to wait before it was answered.

'Can I speak to Detective Frank Thorn, please,' he asked politely. 'It's very important.'

'One moment please,' the returning voice replied and he was placed on hold.

A minute later, the phone was answered. 'Hello, Frank Thorn speaking.'

'Hello Frank. Long time, no see.'

'You,' Frank gasped in reply, recognising the voice straight away. He felt his heart thump in his chest and he glanced out of his office door. Everyone was going about his or her business. He had to try and get someone's attention so that he could get a trace before James rung off. Where the hell was Michelle when he needed her?

DOWN THE STREET FROM THE POLICE STATION

SAME TIME

Once again the government group was using the same building to monitor Frank Thorn's phone lines at work. There were three men sitting at the equipment and in the corner of the room the scarred man himself was standing talking to his personally chosen informant from the police station.

That was the only reason that he was down here himself, because he wanted an update personally.

He believed that Frank Thorn was the group's best chance of re-capturing James and as such was monitoring this part of the operation himself. There were other leads that the group was following up on, but he had delegated these tasks to other people that he could trust.

It was this part that he wanted to be watching because he believed it was only a matter of time.

His source's information this time had not been very helpful. In fact she had nothing of any use to tell him this time. He was just finishing up with her when one of the three men turned round.

'We got him, sir. We're running the trace now. We should have his location very shortly.'

Instantly the scarred man went into action. He grabbed his phone and started to call the people he would need.

He turned round to face his informant and told her to go back to work in the police station so that she didn't raise suspicion. Michelle Gibson nodded a reply but then hesitated.

'One thing,' she asked. 'You want me to keep an eye on Frank but you arranged for me to be partnered with him before James could escape. How did you know?'

'I didn't,' the scarred man replied. 'The group has various sources in various places and I just thought that it might be a good idea to have one of our police sources watching Frank. I had no idea of what was about to happen but on hindsight I would say that it was lucky wouldn't you?'

Michelle nodded a reply, before the scarred man turned and left her to return to work.

FORD RESIDENCE

21:17

The conversation continued between the two men, slowly becoming more and more heated. Frank was running out of patience at trying to get someone's attention to get a trace arranged and he knew that James had probably been on the line longer than he had intended anyway. He wouldn't stay on the line for much longer. He had to keep him talking as long as he could.

'What did you do that warranted M.P.'s being sent out to quarantine that hospital?' he asked him.

'I'll be honest with you, Frank,' James replied slightly sarcastically. 'I really don't have all of the details myself, but that's not important right now. What's important is our little bit of unfinished business.'

'Let me guess,' Frank retorted, his own voice starting to take on a sarcastic edge to it. 'You want to kill me. Is that it? Can't you think of something more original?'

James was a bit taken aback at how quickly he had lost control of the conversation. He countered quickly in retaliation.

'I could kill your wife. How is she anyway? I've seen her you know. I watched her waiting for you to pick her up from work. Did she not tell you how a stranger had commented on her beauty whilst she was waiting?

'She blushed. The blood running to her cheeks. Blood that could easily be spilt. I don't know where you live yet but I do know where you both work. It wouldn't be hard to get to her.'

Frank's sarcasm dropped instantly at the mention of Catherine. 'YOU LAY ONE FINGER ON MY WIFE AND I SWEAR TO GOD I'LL…'

'YOU'LL WHAT?' James shouted back. 'WHAT CAN YOU DO? WHERE CAN YOU HIDE THAT I CAN'T FOLLOW?'

James paused. He heard a car engine switch off. It could be a neighbour's car but it was what he needed to remind him exactly how long he'd been talking to Frank. He could hear the other man saying something in the earpiece. Seconds later he heard the handle of the front door being tried. He smiled. Time to go.

'Listen Frank,' he cut the other man off. 'I'd love to stay and talk but I'm going to have to go. I have guests and their slightly earlier than I would have liked.'

With that he hung up the phone and turned round to face the front door. The handle was being tried again, this time more violently. They'd soon be kicking in the door.

Outside the scarred man stood in the road beside the black van that he'd arrived in with four other men. The men were all dressed in black and were carrying silenced weapons. He didn't want any more attention than he had to. The men were now at the front door to the house where they had traced the phone call. In another few seconds they would be in.

Back in the house, James was now at the front door checking the trap that he'd rigged there. It was ready. He turned and began to run down the hallway and up the stairs. At the top of the stairs he spun round and headed towards a set of stepladders that he'd left set up at the entrance to the attic. He climbed the ladder and pulled himself inside of the attic, kicking over the ladders as he did so.

Downstairs, the front door was finally kicked in and the young man leading the other three men entered. The door opened and snapped support wires that James had rigged. The effect was that a large axe swung down from the ceiling, suspended by the handle with the wiring.

The blade smashed into the chest of the young man, bursting through his ribs, spraying blood and chips of bone outwards. He screamed and collapsed to the floor, writhing in agony. The other three men gave a brief look at their fallen companion and then moved on past him. They had a job to do and they intended to do.

Inside of the attic, James stood waiting; listening to the sound of the screams. He wished that he could have seen the effect of that trap but he knew that he had his own escape to consider. In his hands, he had two glass milk bottles. Both bottles were filled with petrol and had rags stuffed into their necks.

He pulled a lighter out of his pocket and lit the first bottle. Leaning out of the hatch, he threw the bottle at the top of the stairs.

The three men were halfway up the stairs at this point, having already established that the downstairs was empty with the exception of the dead body of the house's owner. The petrol bomb exploded less than a metre in front of them, flames erupting outwards and engulfing everything that it touched. The three men quickly backed off down the stairs before the flames, which were rapidly spreading, could touch them. They had conceded defeat in reaching their quarry this way, but they weren't very keen on facing the scarred man's fury either.

James watched the flames spreading for a few seconds before standing back up in the attic and heading over to the skylight that would lead to the roof. Upon reaching it, he lit the second bottle of petrol and threw it at the entrance of the attic. The flames once again started to spread quickly and eat away at the wooden structures of the roof. James turned back to the skylight and pushed it open to climb out.

In the street below, the three armed men had reached the scarred man again and were reporting their failure.

'He rigged the place,' one of them tried to explain. 'There was no way that we could reach him.'

The scarred man glowered at them, trying hard to keep his temper in check. 'What about Pierce?' he asked referring to the young man who'd been injured by the axe. 'Did you remove his weapons?' The three men nodded a reply, as one.

On the rooftop, James stood watching this. He recognised the scarred man from when he had escaped. By this point there was smoke bellowing out of the skylight and one of the windows in the house shattered from the heat of the fire. He was just about to move off when without warning a spotlight appeared on him from behind. He spun round, shielding his eyes and stepping slightly to his left so that he could see what was happening.

Hovering in mid-air, completely silent was a black helicopter. A spotlight fixed underneath the main body. It began to lower itself to the same level as James. The wind it was kicking up was blowing the smoke about further and whipping James's hair about.

James was stunned. He'd read about these black helicopters in U.F.O. stories, but he'd never thought that they actually existed. At a distance you probably couldn't even see it and if the stories were to be believed then it was probably stealth.

The flames and smoke were starting to get the attention of the neighbours, some of whom were venturing out of their houses for a closer look at what was going on.

Back on the ground, a radio that the scarred man was holding in his hand crackled to life. 'Subject is on the roof,' came the report from the helicopter.

The scarred man glanced around at some of the watching neighbours. Normally he wouldn't allow the group to get so much exposure but they were running out of time to find a cure for this virus. Already, he'd heard of two cases of infection out with the hospital. He had to press on and try and capture James now.

'Take the subject down, but don't kill him. Do I make myself clear?' he ordered into the radio.

'Yes. Sir,' came the reply.

The side door of the helicopter opened and a sniper came forward from the inside shadows. He levelled his rifle and decided to take a few warning shots first. He aimed and fired. The bullet hit a tile just inches away from James's foot.

This was enough to get James to spring to action. His escape plan falling to bits, he turned and started to run across the slanting rooftop as fast as he could safely do it. From one house rooftop to the next he moved away from the helicopter. The tiles that he was stepping on were breaking and slipping out from under his feet, sliding down into the guttering at the edge of the rooftop.

James almost lost his footing but was able to grab hold of a television aerial connected to someone's chimney. Two more bullets smashed into the roof followed by an amplified voice.

'JAMES BLACK. THESE ARE WARNING SHOTS ONLY. SURRENDER NOW OR THE NEXT ONE WILL HIT YOU.'

James turned round to face the helicopter, his face twisted into a snarl, feeling defenceless and cornered.

He turned back again and leapt over the apex of the roof. The sniper didn't give any more warning and fired again. The bullet hit James in the leg as he was landing on the other side. He twisted in pain and his landing messed up. He fell onto his back and the tiles started to give way under him. They started to slide down the rooftop, taking him along with them. He slid towards the edge picking up speed as he went. More and more tiles were spraying off the edge of the roof.

He braced himself for reaching the edge. His hope was that if he could wedge his feet into the guttering when he got there, he wouldn't slide of the roof. Instead when his feet hit, the gutter was wrenched from its fittings in the wall and he slid off the rooftop, plunging down into the pile of tiles below.

At the front of the house, the scarred man ordered the three men from the failed mission in the house to go round to the relevant back garden and capture James whilst they still could.

The helicopter swung its spotlight around to try and locate the fallen killer but was having no luck.

'Unable to find target,' the pilot reported into his radio.

In the street, the first of the police cars and fire engines could be heard in the distance.

'Get out of here,' the scarred man ordered into the radio. The helicopter was no use if it couldn't find James. There was no need in unnecessary exposure. The spotlight blinked out and the helicopter was almost straight away invisible in the night sky.

Changing frequencies, the scarred man started to speak into his radio again. 'Anything,' he asked.

In the back garden, the three men stood looking at the pile of broken tiles. There was no sign of James but there was a faint trail of blood.

'He's gone,' one of the men replied to the scarred man through his radio.

'Pull out and return to base,' the scarred man ordered.

'We can track him sir,' the reply came.

'NO. He'd only kill you one by one. We've lost the element of surprise. He'd be waiting. He did enough damage to us when we did have surprise on our side. Now, you have your orders. Follow them.'

The scarred man pulled back and disappeared into the crowd that was forming in the street. The first police cars, fire engines and an ambulance had now actually arrived. He would leave the van that they'd arrived in for the police to do whatever they wanted with it. There was nothing in the van to lead them back to the group.

Several streets away, James moved through garden after garden. He was walking at quite a fast pace. His leg was hurting like hell and his body was racked with pain from the fall but he was confident that by tomorrow it would be mostly away. The worst would be that his leg would throb a bit. He still had to pull the bullet out when he got a chance, but first he had to get to safety.

His suspicions about the group coming to get him were right, but he'd underestimated the tools at their disposal. The man who had the scar running down his cheek was proving to be troublesome. If he wanted him so bad, then that was exactly what he would get. Then maybe the entire group would take the warning and leave him to his own devices.

SECRET UNDERGROUND INSTALLATION

EDINBURGH

02:03

'Our initial attempt to re-capture James Black has failed,' the scarred man reported to the group of men who were all sitting round a large table. 'We will get him the next time.'

'I hope for all our sakes that you're right,' the elderly man sighed. 'I was informed a little over twenty minutes ago that there has been three new cases of infection of the virus, one of them in Glasgow. It is getting out of control.

'It also begs the question of how many cases are not getting reported due to people not going to their doctors. It is very likely that the total number of cases is much higher.'

With that the elderly man got up from the table that he was sitting at and left the room, his mind already resigning itself for what he believed the inevitable outcome of all this would be. The destruction of Mankind.

POLICE STATION

10:11

Frank sat at his desk, a local newspaper between his hands. It was turned to a page about an arson attack on an Edinburgh man's home. The paper held reports of a black helicopter and of a chase along the rooftops of the houses in the area. The authorities had denied the reports of the helicopters, saying that there was no evidence of them.

'That was you, wasn't it?' Frank muttered under his breath. Standing up abruptly, he left the office to try and find out who was in charge of the fire incident. He would pursue the Black case on his own if he had to.

FOUR DAYS LATER

OUTSIDE ENTRANCE TO SECRET UNDERGROUND INSTALLATION

19:57

James sat in a car at the side of the road. He'd been there all day, watching the gates at the end of the alleyway where he had escaped. The car that he was in was stolen but he didn't have to worry about the owner reporting it stolen any time soon. He had killed her and her body was currently in the boot. He was waiting for the scarred man to leave. He didn't know how long it would take but he wasn't in any hurry.

Just then as if on cue, the scarred man appeared and left the gateway, heading across the street towards what James assumed was his car. He watched as the scarred man's car pulled away and started his own car. He started to follow, keeping at least one car between them at all times.

SCARRED MAN'S RESIDENCE

23:31

The scarred man stood at his small bar that was situated in the corner of his living room. He dropped two ice cubes into the glass of whiskey that he had just poured himself. His other hand held his cordless phone to his ear. He was listening to a routine report from one of his men. A few minutes later he had heard it all and thanked the operative before hanging up.

The news wasn't good. After four days there had been no more signs of James Black. He hadn't made any more contact with Frank or if he had it hadn't been via the phone. There was now more than thirty cases of the virus that the group knew of.

Suddenly he had an idea. He picked up his phone again, dialled the number and placed it to his ear. It started to ring but before it could be answered the line suddenly went dead. 'What the hell,' the scarred man muttered. He barely had time to register this when he heard a faint noise from his kitchen.

Putting his drink onto the bar top, he marched over to his desk. Upon reaching it, he opened the drawer and pulled out a gun. If there was an intruder, then they would regret the day that they broke into his house, he'd make damn sure of it.

He removed the safety from the gun and headed through towards the kitchen. With the gun held ready, the scarred man spun round the doorframe, his left hand flicking on the light switch as he did so. The kitchen was empty. The back door however was swinging open. Somebody was indeed in his home. He walked over to the back door and closed it again, locking it as he did so, the keys hanging out of the lock. He now needed to check his whole house.

Moving from room to room, switching on the lights as he went, the scarred man checked the whole house. Looking in all of the spaces that someone could possibly hide. His house was empty. He went back into the kitchen trying to work out what was going on.

Abruptly the house was plunged into darkness. The scarred man felt the first traces of uncertainty entering his mind. With an effort he forced himself to calm down and think. He had a flashlight in one of the kitchen cupboards. He was also getting a little illumination from moonlight through the kitchen window. He began to feel his way along the kitchen units until he reached the one that he was looking for. He opened the door and started to grope around inside for his torch, finding it a few seconds later.

Turning the torch on, the beam of light lanced through the darkness. He swung it round to re-check the shadows of the room, where the moonlight wasn't reaching. Still there was nobody there.

From the direction of the living room, there came the sound of shattering glass. The scarred man's heart missed a beat in fright. Gritting his teeth he began to march through towards the living room. The torch held in one hand and the gun in the other. Reaching the living room, he swung the torch around so that the beam of light lit the dark room up. A large glass table that sat in the middle of his living room was smashed and lying in pieces on his carpet. Other than that he couldn't see anything out of place.

There was a thump from the hallway and despite himself the scarred man could start to feel his uncertainty turn into the first traces of fear. A thought occurred to him. He could just leave the house right now and go to one of his neighbour's houses to call the police or better still the group. No sooner had he thought this, than his pride piped up. He couldn't do that. He'd never live it down. There came another thump from the hallway.

The scarred man started to move out of the living room to investigate further, pushing his fear to the back of his mind. He swung the beam of light in the direction of the noise. There was still nothing. The light from the torch made the shadows behind him and on either side of him seem even darker. The darkness was pressing in, threatening to drown him. There came another noise from behind him.

He swung round, gun and torch held out. Once again there was nothing there. What the hell was going on? Suddenly he felt himself being grabbed from behind. The fright caused him to drop both the gun and the torch. The torch fell to the ground and started to roll along the floor. The beam of light rolled with the torch, illuminating the struggle and projecting shadows onto the far wall.

James swung the scarred man around, throwing him to the floor at the same time. The scarred man started to call out for help; all thoughts of his pride being dented had left his mind. He scrambled to his feet and started to run through to the kitchen and the back door. James stood calmly watching him.

When the scarred man reached the door, he froze. The keys that he'd left in the door just minutes earlier were gone. He could hear the footsteps of the other man as he entered the kitchen.

'Looking for something?' James called from behind the scarred man, followed by the jingling of keys.

Trapped, the scared man turned round to face James. His fear was turning into anger at his predicament. 'YOU BASTARD,' he shouted before lunging across the room at James.

The killer stood his ground and watched as the scarred man approached. At the exact moment, he swung his right hand up and grabbed the scarred man by the throat, his hand like a vice, he started to squeeze.

The scarred man started to struggle for air, kicking out at his attacker as he did so. James ignored the blows and threw the scarred man against the wall-mounted cupboards. The scarred man hit the cupboards and fell to the floor. The impact stunned him slightly. James walked over to him and kicked him in the face breaking his nose.

He reached down and grabbed the scarred man's throat again, pulling him back to his feet. With his other hand, James pulled his knife from its sheath, and before the scarred man could even register what was happening, James plunged it into his opponent's stomach, twisting it round in an anti-clockwise direction. The blood began to spill out onto the floor, looking black in the moonlight.

Pulling the knife free again, James threw the scarred man down to the floor. He wasn't done with him yet. He had to make an example of him so that hopefully this group of men, whoever they were would leave him alone.

SCARRED MAN'S RESIDENCE

00:43

James got back up from beside the body of the scarred man who was now very dead. He was covered in blood but that didn't matter. The scarred man had had his face literally cut off and he had been gutted. His insides scattered around the kitchen.

James left the kitchen and walked back into the hallway. He was about to leave when he saw the scarred man's gun in the beam of light from the fallen torch. He bent down to retrieve it. It might come in handy later on.

With that done, he reached the front door, unlocked it and left the house, leaving the door swinging open.

SECRET UNDERGROUND INSTALLATION

09:14

The elderly man sat on his own at his desk. In front of him were photos from the house of the scarred man. He might not have always seen eye to eye with him, but what had happened to him last night, he wouldn't have wished on anyone.

The death of the scarred man had shocked even him. The message that James had wanted to put over by killing the scarred man was quite clear, but they still needed him. Yes they had their scientists working on a cure but they had been trying that since World War 2 and were still no closer. That was why they had hoped that James would provide the cure for them and it was also why they had to keep trying to capture him again.

FORTH ROAD BRIDGE

11:29

James got out of the car, closing the door behind him. He'd driven as close as he could. In front of his car were two waist high barriers. They were covered in barbwire to put people off from moving them and or climbing over them. A sign was attached to one of the barriers. It read:

DANGER

KEEP OFF BRIDGE

Ignoring the sign, James slid past the barriers and started to walk down the deserted Road Bridge. To his right, he could see the rail bridge.

He stopped beside the one and only remaining tower. Scaffolding was erected around it. Upon closer inspection, James found a rusting service ladder running up one side of the tower. In the distance he could see that the bridge now ended in a sheer drop, well short of the landfall it used to make.

The bridge swayed in the wind, the metal groaning. James looked up, there was a storm coming but that wouldn't interfere with his plans.

This was the place, he decided. It was here that he'd sworn his revenge and it was here that he would get it. He'd bring Frank here and they would both remember that fateful day. He closed his eyes, feeling the ice wind against his face.

In his mind's eye he remembered everything that had happened that evening. How he nearly escaped, the shock and pain of the bullet, the icy sea below, his burning desire for revenge and something else about Frank that he couldn't quite place. Still couldn't place.

He opened his eyes again. That was all in the past and he had to think about the present. He needed bait to get Frank here. He started to walk back to his car.

POLICE STATION

21:33

Frank sat at his desk looking over police reports. He was working on the Black case unofficially. He had gone to Detective Paul Bond to get some of the files that he needed concerning the house fire several nights earlier and the murder of some man who the police had yet to put a name to, but the police had been able to pull finger prints off that crime scene and they had been matched to James Black. Finally people believed him. However he wasn't put on the case. He was told he was too close to it, so he was working on it unofficially.

The door to his office opened and Michelle walked in holding a manila envelope.

'Someone left this at the desk for you,' she said as she handed it to him. 'It's marked urgent.'

Frank took and opened it, tipping the contents out onto his desk. Two Polaroid photos and a piece of paper fell out. He turned them over to look at them. The pictures were of his wife Catherine. She was tied up and gagged. The note read:

Forth road bridge by 10:30pm or she dies. You can bring your sceptical partner if you want but anyone else and she dies.

Frank felt the blood drain from his face. 'Oh God, no,' he muttered. He reached out and grabbed his phone, dialling his home number. 'Please answer,' he muttered. When there came no answer, he slammed the phone down in the cradle.

'What's wrong?' Michelle asked.

'The son of a bitch has my wife,' he replied as he got up from his desk. 'Come on, I need your help.'

'I'll be right with you,' she called out to him as he headed away from her, his mind set on getting Catherine back.

Michelle then glanced at the photos and the note, before pulling her mobile phone out. She started walking after Frank. She wouldn't lose him. He needed her help after all. Her commitment to the group didn't stop her from honouring her commitment to her partner, after all it was James Black that the group was after not Frank.

SECRET UNDERGROUND INSTALLATION

21:39

One of the more senior members of the group approached the elderly man to report to him that Michelle Gibson had phoned in and said that James Black was currently on the old Forth Road Bridge and that he'll probably be there until about half ten.

'Well done,' the elderly man replied. He reached over and picked up his phone. He issued his security password and got through to the department that he was wanting.

'Prep one of the helicopters now. I'll be there in about twenty minutes. I want it ready by then. No later.'

FORTH ROAD BRIDGE

21:46

James stood at the half way point of the bridge. He was looking over at Fife. The end of the bridge that was on that side was completely missing. It was strange to look at. He turned and started to walk back towards the Edinburgh end and Catherine who was tied up near the beginning of the bridge

He had waited for her to leave work and had grabbed her there and now it was just a question of waiting. He reached her and knelt down beside her. 'If your husband gets here on time, you'll walk out of here alive, I promise you that. If not you die.'

Catherine glared at him, unable to answer due to her gag.

MILITARY AIR BASE

EDINBURGH

21:57

The elderly man climbed into the back of the helicopter. Already waiting inside was the pilot and a government sniper.

'Let's go,' the elderly man ordered.

Without any sound at all the helicopter began to rise off the ground and head towards its destination.

FORTH ROAD BRIDGE

21:58

Frank floored the accelerator as he approached the bridge. He passed the remains of the old tollbooths and he could see the two barriers blocking the way ahead but still he didn't slow down.

'Frank,' Michelle started but was silenced by the fierce look that he shot her.

James stood on the bridge watching the approaching vehicle. A smile spread across his face. 'Time to play,' he muttered.

There was a high-pitched screech as the car's brakes were applied at the last moment. The car skidded into the two barbwire barriers and knocked them over. They slid across the concrete for a couple of metres.

The car door was open before the car was even at a standstill, Frank leaping out. 'CATHERINE,' he shouted.

'She's alive,' James replied for her. He was walking towards Frank. Frank saw his wife's form lying on the ground behind James and tried to swerve past the killer to get to her.

James anticipated this and grabbed hold of Frank's arm as he tried to pass. He shoved Frank against the railing hard, his other hand pulling out his knife from its sheath.

With his mind fully on killing Frank, James forgot about the other passenger in the car. Michelle was by this time out of the car and approaching James and Frank. The group might well want James but she wasn't going to just stand and let him kill her partner.

James heard the footsteps at the last possible moment and turned round, in time to see Michelle's fist as it hit him squarely in the face. He staggered back from the blow, dropping the knife and releasing his grip on Frank as he did so.

Frank took the chance to go to his wife. Grabbing the killer's fallen knife, he scrambled over to her. Checking her pulse to ensure that she was indeed alive, he began to cut the ropes that were binding her.

Meanwhile James was advancing towards Michelle. 'You'll pay for that, bitch,' he threatened. The distance between them was closing. Michelle however stood her ground.

When he was within reach, Michelle swung her fist at him again. This time James was ready and with no effort at all he caught her fist mid-swing. He wrenched it back and there was a splintering sound as her wrist broke. Less than a second later the broken bone fragment burst through her skin, spraying a fine mist of red blood. Michelle screamed and tried to fall away from him.

The scream got Frank's attention. 'Michelle,' he shouted as he got back up from beside Catherine and rushed to help his partner, the knife still in his hand.

James threw Michelle into one of the fallen barbwire barriers. She landed on it and felt the barbs tear through her flesh, her clothes providing no protection at all. She continued to scream out in pain and tried to raise herself back off of the barrier with her one good hand.

Frank reached James and plunged the knife into his side. James twisted away from the attack and the blade slid back out of the wound. Frank still held onto the knife, as it was his only weapon against the killer.

James put his hand down to the cut in his side and felt the blood running over his hands. 'Well done,' he said to Frank. 'Didn't see that coming, but you're going to regret it.'

Before Frank could make another lunge, James lashed out at him. His punch hitting him square in the face knocking him down to the concrete road.

With Frank lying on the ground, James turned back to finish off Michelle. She was struggling to get back up again and had only succeeded in getting her upper half of her torso raised as she only had one good hand. Every move causing her more pain as the barbs from the barrier tore into her.

James raised his boot and pushed it against the back of Michelle's head forcing it back down into the barbwire. Michelle cried out in protest and pain. She tried to hold her head up against his foot but she didn't have the strength. Her face was getting closer and closer to the barbs and there was nothing that she could do to stop it. With one final push of his boot, James forced her head right down into the barbwire. Michelle felt her face being torn apart by the barbs. One of her eyes burst as one of the barbs pressed in against it and she felt the eye fluid running down her face. James continued to push down until he could push no further. The screams finally stopped.

Frank was getting back to his feet, too late to do anything to stop him from killing his partner. 'YOU SICK BASTARD,' he shouted at him, grabbing hold of the knife which he had dropped when he was punched to the ground.

James spun round to face both Frank and Catherine. 'YOU,' he shouted at Catherine. 'GET OUT OF HERE.'

Catherine stood defiant. 'NO,' she shouted back. 'I WILL NOT LEAVE MY HUSBAND.'

James reached round his side to the small of his back where he had tucked the gun, which he had taken from the scarred man's house, into his belt. He pulled it out and pointed it at her. 'GO NOW,' he ordered. 'OR DIE. YOUR CHOICE.'

Despite herself, Catherine's resolve buckled and fell to pieces. She started to edge along the bridge past James to safety. James ignored her, only interested in Frank.

Above them came the first peal of thunder and the wind started to pick up. James considered just shooting Frank, but where was the fun in that. He pushed the gun back into his belt.

'COME ON FRANK,' he challenged. 'COME ON AND FACE ME.'

Frank saw that his wife was safely off of the bridge entirely but didn't want to run the risk of James turning his attention back on to her. He had to keep his attention. With that in mind he turned and ran.

With half the bridge missing he had nowhere to go however. He swerved towards one of the towers. Clamping the knife blade between his teeth, he started to climb the rusting service ladder that ran up the side of the tower. He was hoping that James wouldn't be so keen to follow him.

James stood watching as Frank ran away from his challenge. 'Coward,' he muttered under his breath, before following. Reaching the ladder, he too started to climb.

The wind was whistling overhead and picking up. The first drops of rain started to fall and there was another crash of thunder. The tower creaked and groaned as the winds hit it. It began to sway slightly in the wind as the storm started to pick up. Still the two men continued to climb. Higher and higher, they went. The top getting closer and closer. Frank passed the top level of the supporting scaffolding and continued up for another fifteen feet or so to the top of the tower itself.

Frank started to pull himself onto the horizontal platform that linked the two vertical sections of the tower. Lying on his stomach he began to crawl along the platform. His arms and legs ached with fatigue. The tower was rusted to hell and the metal creaking underneath him didn't help boost his confidence. He reached the opposite vertical support and looked over the side, hoping to find another ladder so that he could get back down. No such luck. This side didn't have a ladder, just a straight drop down. Cursing himself, he began to turn himself around to face the way that he had come.

Meanwhile, James had now reached the top and was getting to his feet. He stood to his full height, despite the strong winds battering against him. The only thing separating the two men now was the horizontal platform. James started to walk forward, closing the gap slowly but surely.

Realising that he was trapped, Frank began to stand up as well to meet the challenge. He pulled the knife out from between his teeth and readied himself for what he now knew was probably going to be the last few minutes of his life. The sky above them lit up with lightening followed seconds later by a huge peal of thunder.

When the gap between the men was less than a metre, Frank lunged. At the same time another strong gust of wind hit, catching Frank and knocking him over. He reached out and grabbed hold of James. Both men toppled over the edge, only to land on the top level of the scaffolding fifteen feet below. The wooden planks that they landed on cracked but held never the less. The knife fell from Frank's hand and lay forgotten about.

The two men grappled with each other, landing punch after punch on top of each other. Frank tried to aim for the knife wound in James's side to maximise the effect that his attack would have. James retaliated with a more violent attack of his own. Both men were so determined to outdo the other that neither of them saw the black helicopter silently approach.

Inside of the helicopter, the elderly man ordered the pilot to hover level with the tower. The side door to the helicopter was opened and the elderly man raised a voice amplifier to his mouth.

'JAMES BLACK,' he called.

Across from him on top of the scaffolding, the two men froze, their attention drawn to the new arrival.

Frank began to pull away from James in an effort to catch his breath. Meanwhile James got back to his feet, glaring at the helicopter, already knowing that it was the group of men who had held him for so long. They obviously hadn't taken his warning when he had killed the scarred man

'JAMES,' the elderly man repeated. 'WE'RE NOT HERE TO TRY AND CAPTURE YOU AGAIN...'

'WHAT MAKES YOU THINK THAT YOU COULD?' James cut him off. The elderly man ignored this remark. 'WE NEED YOUR HELP,' he continued to press. 'THAT SYRINGE THAT YOU TOOK CONTAINED A VIRUS THAT WE HAVE NO CURE FOR. NOW THAT YOU'VE RELEASED IT WE NEED A CURE FAST. IF YOU WOULD LET US USE YOUR DNA TO HELP US FIND A CURE, I PROMISE YOU THAT YOU WILL BE RELEASED AS SOON AS WE'RE DONE.'

'WHY ME?' James asked.

'YOU SHOULD KNOW BY NOW. YOU'RE THE RESULT OF A GENETIC EXPERIMENT. THAT'S WHY YOU'VE SURVIVED SO MUCH AND WHY YOU'RE ALIVE TODAY.

'YOU'RE BODY IS IMMUNE TO ALL DISEASES AND CAN HEAL ITSELF MUCH FASTER THAN A NORMAL MAN'S COULD.'

Frank had heard enough. He hadn't gone through the hell of the last nine years to let James slip through again. He searched around, finding the knife lying a little to his left. He reached out for it, checking to see if he had been noticed. He needn't have bothered. Everybody's attention was on what was happening between James and the man in the helicopter. It was time to finish James off once and for all, or die trying. He didn't care what this man in the helicopter said about James being able to heal faster. No one lived forever. He took a deep breath and scrambled to his feet, charging at James.

James saw the movement out of the corner of his eye. He began to turn around but he was too late. Frank reached him and plunged the knife into the killer's chest. This being made easier by James turning round to face whatever was coming. The blade of the knife burst through, sliding in between two ribs and stabbing into the killer's heart.

'NO,' the elderly man shouted as Frank pushed the blade in deeper.

'Take him down,' the elderly man ordered the sniper in the back with him. The sniper levelled his rifle at Frank, aimed and fired. The bullet hit Frank in the back of the head, killing him instantly and spraying James's face with blood and chips of bone. Frank's body collapsed onto the scaffolding.

James stood stock still. The knife was still jutting out from his chest. He was in a slight state of shock at what had just happened. He coughed a spray of blood from his mouth and his body began to sway in the wind.

The elderly man raised the voice amplifier to his mouth again.

'JAMES,' he started. 'A NORMAL MAN WOULD BE DEAD BY NOW, HOWEVER EVEN YOUR HEALING POWERS CAN'T SAVE YOU THIS TIME. UNLESS YOU GET MEDICAL ATTENTION, YOU'LL BE DEAD IN LESS THAN AN HOUR.

'COME WITH US. WE'LL SAVE YOUR LIFE, FIND OUR CURE, IF ONE CAN BE FOUND AND THEN RELEASE YOU. IT'S YOU'RE ONLY CHANCE. YOU MUST TRUST ME. PLEASE.'

James felt his legs buckle under his weight and he fell to his knees. His vision was becoming blurry and black patches were appearing. He blinked them away. Should he trust this man? He considered it and decided to take his chances.

He began to reach behind his back for the gun that he'd shoved back there. The elderly man narrowed his eyes to try and make out what he was doing.

'NO,' James shouted his answer, pulling the gun out as he did so. He blinked the black patches away and for a second, his sight was perfect again. It was all he needed. He aimed and fired.

'Pull up,' the elderly man ordered but it was too late. The bullet smashed through the glass in the front of the helicopter, hitting the pilot in the chest, who slumped forward against the controls. The helicopter spun round and started to nose dive as it did, straight towards James and the bridge tower.

James was now on the verge of passing out and so didn't see the effect that killing the pilot had.

A second later the blades hit the steel tower and the entire section was engulfed in a massive fireball. The already weakened upper half of the tower tore away under the impact and explosion, the remaining steel cables finally snapping under the pressure. The tower plunged down to the ground below, pulling a large number of support scaffolding down with it. The whole bridge started to shake and even as the fiery debris started to land, the main bulk of the bridge started to collapse into the sea.

TWO DAYS LATER

13:10

Damien Lee started to walk down the street. His mind was playing over the events of the last few days, since the group had learned of the death of both their leader and of James Black. The virus continued to spread, but the group had descended into squabbling over who should be in charge instead of uniting against the common threat.

So far only one of the bodies had been recovered from the wreckage, but that wasn't important anymore. What mattered was trying to find a cure to the virus, which was now so unlikely, but Damien wouldn't give up. He'd find a way otherwise; Mankind would have entered the last stage of his evolution – the beginning of the end.

PURE EVIL UNLEASHED…

A VIRUS WITH NO CURE…

A HIDDEN GOVERNMENT…

AN UNSPEAKABLE WAR…

MANKIND FACING EXTINCTION…

GENOCIDE

COMING SOON.

Read an extract from *Genocide I: Evil Never Dies* on the following pages.

www.adamshiels.com

SEPTEMBER IN THE NEAR FUTURE

SOUTH QUEENSFERRY

(OUTSKIRTS OF EDINBURGH)

01:34

The rain clouds rolled across the dark night sky. The wind hammered against the desolate buildings standing across from the pier. The sea was practically alive as it crashed against the stonewall of the harbour, spraying salt water over the railings. A flickering street lamp shone its orange glow onto the building shells.

Less than a decade earlier the buildings had housed successful businesses, now they lay empty and at the mercy of the elements.

Inside of the remains of one of the buildings, Stuart White and Ben Crow sat huddled up in blankets for warmth. Both men were filthy and unshaven as only the truly homeless can be. In the middle of the stone floor, a small fire crackled giving some heat and comfort but not much.

Outside, David Ford staggered against the wind towards the building that his two companions were inside of. He stopped to take a drink from the large bottle that he was carrying. A strong gust of wind hit him, causing him to stagger forwards and drop the bottle. It hit the pavement, shattering on impact, the contents forming a small river into the gutter.

'Shit,' he muttered under his breath. Nothing ever went right for him. The first drops of rain started as if to confirm that thought. Pulling the collar of his tatty old coat up, he started back towards the abandoned building.

The flickering streetlamp in front of him went out completely for a few seconds before bursting back to life. David froze. Standing in front of him was a man. He hadn't been there a few seconds earlier. The figure stood motionless, the upper half of it's body hidden in the shadows.

'Hello?' David slurred cautiously. There came no reply.

'Who is that?' David demanded. Still no answer came. The figure began to move towards him, the upper half of the body moving into the light from the streetlamp. The figure wore black overalls, it's skin was deathly pale, tainted orange by the light.

David was about to issue a warning not to get any closer, but just then the figure's face was exposed entirely by the streetlight. His warning died away on his lips. The figure's eyes were jet black. No whites, no pupils, just a jet-black swirling emptiness.

'Oh my God,' David muttered, before turning and running.

The figure started after him, not running but seeming to close to distance never the less.

'HELP,' David called out. 'SOMEONE PLEASE HELP ME.'

Without warning the figure's hands grabbed him from behind and threw him against the wall of a nearby building. He hit it with a thump. The shock of the impact coupled with the drink that he'd had, slowed his reactions down and he wasn't able to get back up to his feet fast enough to escape the approaching figure. He opened his mouth and screamed.

Inside of the building that he had been heading to, his two companions stood up hearing the screaming. Even over the wind they could hear it.

'Is that David?' Ben asked. Without waiting for an answer his companion headed out of the door into the wind and rain. Ben followed suit.

Once outside they began to call out for their friend. 'DAVID,' they shouted together. The sound was carried by the wind as the storm increased. The rain was now lashing down.

They continued to walk and call out for their companion as they went. Still they got no reply. Without warning a hand shot out from the shadows of a dark alleyway between two of the buildings. Both Stuart and Ben screamed in fright and started to back away.

'Help me,' came a weak voice from the alley. 'Please.'

The two men recognised the voice. It belonged to their missing friend. As if to prove the point, David staggered from the alleyway into the flickering light. His face was covered in blood and he was holding his hands out for help.

Ben and Stuart both started forward to offer help but froze when they saw the shape of the figure approaching from behind David.

Upon reaching David, the figure grabbed his throat from behind and started to dig its nails into the flesh, forcing it's fingers through fat, blood and tissue. Having literally established a grip on David's windpipe, the figure wrenched its hand away, ripping the windpipe out from David's throat with a sickening squelching sound.

David fell to the pavement, his blood starting to pool around him and run into the gutter with the rainwater.

Both Ben and Stuart, who had been frozen to the spot until this point, turned and ran. The figure started after them. Around them the storm continued to rage. A powerful wave hit the harbour wall, spraying the men above with salt water. The two men ignored it and continued to run.

Stuart turned to look over his shoulder as he ran. The figure was gone. He slowed down and stopped running. Where had it gone?

'Ben,' he shouted. 'Ben. Stop. He's gone.'

Ben stopped and turned round to face Stuart, gasping for air as he did so

'Where'd he go?' he asked.

Stuart was about to answer when a pair of hands reached round from behind him. Ben didn't even have time to issue a warning to his friend before the figure had a grip on both Stuart's chin and his shoulder. Twisting its hands in opposite directions, it snapped Stuart's neck with no effort at all and threw his body down to the ground.

Despite the fear surging through Ben, he wasn't able to move from the spot he was standing on. He could only watch as the figure approached him.

It wasn't until the figure had a hold on him, that Ben actually tried to escape but by then it was too late. The figure held Ben's arms tight against his side and with no effort at all, it picked Ben up like a child would a rag doll. Its face remaining completely expressionless as it carried Ben towards the metal railings that ran along the harbour wall.

Ben started to beg for his life, trying to find a way to reason with it. Instead, all he got was the blank expressionless look of the figure's black swirling eyes.

Upon reaching the railings, the figure raised Ben above it's head and brought him down hard against the top rail. Ben's back took the full force of the impact. There came a loud crack as his spine broke.

Ben howled, suddenly unable to feel his lower body or kick out in self-defence. He began to pray in between his moan.

The figure once again lifted Ben above its head and threw him into the choppy sea below. The ice-cold water hit Ben like a brick. Unable to use his legs to help him swim, he tried to keep afloat with his arms alone. The stormy waters were too much for him however and he was quickly forced under the surface. He re-doubled his efforts to keep afloat and managed to get back to the surface for a brief second to get one last gasp of air. The effort to do this however, exhausted him and he was back under again in a matter of seconds. Salt water flooded his mouth as he tried in vain to get air. Within seconds his lungs began to start filling up with seawater.

The figure stood at the railing, watching as the human struggled for a few more minutes and once it was satisfied that he was dead, it turned and started to walk away. It had something that it needed to do.

www.ingramcontent.com/pod-product-compliance
Ingram Content Group UK Ltd.
Pitfield, Milton Keynes, MK11 3LW, UK
UKHW041942190726
13854UKWH00004B/1734